RUBBED OUT

a John Wads Crime Novella
book 2

JERRY PETERSON

This book is a work of fiction. Names, characters, places and incidents are the products of the author's imagination or are used fictitiously. All characters in this book have no existence outside the imagination of the author and have no relationship to anyone, living or dead, bearing the same name or names. All incidents are pure invention from the author's imagination. Any resemblance to actual events or locales or persons, living or dead, is entirely coincidental.

All Rights Reserved. Except for use in any review, the reproduction or utilization of this work in whole or in part in any form by any electronic, mechanical or other means, now known or hereafter invented, including xerography, photocopying or recording, or in any information or retrieval system, is forbidden without the prior written permission of both the publisher and copyright owner of this book.

Copyright 2014 c Jerry Peterson
Grand Medallion Books

All Rights Reserved.

ISBN-13: 978-150-2959645
ISBN-10: 150295964X

Cover Design c Dawn Charles at bookgraphics.wordpress.com

November 2014

Printed in the U.S.A.

DEDICATION

To Marge, my wife and first reader.

To the members of my writers group, *Tuesdays with Story*, sharp-eyed readers and writers who demand the very best of me in my storytelling and craft of writing.

To a friend and one-time colleague who prefers to remain unnamed.

ACKNOWLEDGMENTS

This is the eleventh book I've published as indie author, the fifth under my Grand Medallion Books imprint.

We indies, loners that we are, nonetheless depend on a lot of people to make our stories and books the best that they can be. Dawn Charles of Book Graphics, a superb cover designer, worked with me on this volume, as she has on several previous books.

Just as a knock-out cover is vital to grabbing potential readers, so are the words on the back cover that say this book is one you really should buy and read tonight. For those words, I turned to a fellow Wisconsin writer, Betsy Draine. Betsy writes with her partner, Michael Hinden. If you're not acquainted with their work, I suggest you read their latest Nora Barnes and Toby Sandler mystery, *The Body in Bodega Bay*. It's a good one.

I always close with a note of appreciation to all librarians around the country. They, like you and your fellow readers who have enjoyed my James Early mysteries, my AJ Garrison crime novels, my John Wads crime novellas, my Wings Over the Mountains novels, and my short story collections have been real boosters. Without them and you, there would be no reason to write.

A NOTE FROM THE AUTHOR

I launched my John Wads crime novella series earlier this years with *Iced*, a thriller . . . short chapters, tightly written, a fast, fast read.

Rubbed Out is a step back toward the traditional mystery. Still with short chapters. Still tightly written. But the book is longer, in round figures 30,000 words, 50 percent longer than *Iced*.

The idea for this novella came last spring when Marge and I swung off the road in Missouri to see Fantastic Caverns. Neither of us had been there before. It was a brochure we had picked up at a tourist information stop that sold us. The brochure advertised Fantastic Caverns as "America's only ride-through cave."

We jumped on a Jeep-drawn tram, and a guide drove us inside, down through the cave to a turn-around point, and back out, telling us about the sights all the way along . . . a 55-minute tour.

Back in Prohibition days, the owner operated a speakeasy in this cave.

Crank forward to the 1950s and '60s. The owner hosted a series of Grand Ole Opry type shows, the performers working from a stage in the cave, and the shows broadcast live on local radio station KGBX.

A big cave, a speakeasy, a performance space for music shows . . . throw in a little crime and corruption and, wow, the story possibilities are terrific.

The result, *Rubbed Out.*

Enjoy.

JP
Janesville, Wisconsin, November 2014

ALSO BY JERRY PETERSON

Early's Fall, a James Early Mystery, book 1 . . . "If James Early were on the screen instead of in a book, no one would leave the room."
– Robert W. Walker, author of *Children of Salem*

Early's Winter, a James Early Mystery, book 2 . . . "Jerry Peterson's *Early's Winter* is a fine tale for any season. A little bit Western, a little bit mystery, all add up to a fast-paced, well-written novel that has as much heart as it does darkness. Peterson is a first-rate storyteller. Give *Early's Winter* a try, and I promise you, you'll be begging for the next James Early novel. Spring can't come too soon."
– Larry D. Sweazy, Spur-award winning author of *The Badger's Revenge*

The Watch, an AJ Garrison Crime Novel, book 1 . . . "Jerry Peterson has written a terrific mystery, rich in atmosphere of place and time. New lawyer A.J. Garrison is a smart, gutsy heroine."
– James Mitchell, author of *Our Lady of the North*

Rage, an AJ Garrison Crime Novel, book 2 . . . "Terrifying. Just–terrifying. Timely and profound and

even heartbreaking. Peterson's taut spare style and truly original voice create a high-tension page turner. I really loved this book."
– Hank Phillippi Ryan, Agatha, Anthony and Macavity winning author

The Last Good Man, a Wings Over the Mountains novel, Book 1 . . . Jerry Peterson joins the ranks of the writer's writer–that is, an author other authors can learn from, as in how to open and close a book, but also in how to run the course."
– Robert W. Walker, author of *Curse of the RMS Titanic*

Capitol Crime, a Wings Over the Mountains novel, Book 2 . . . "In *Capitol Crime*, Peterson's vivid characters jump right off the page, and his sharp detail and snappy dialog puts the reader right in the middle of Prohibition-era action and one of the wildest schemes ever to take down a bootlegging ring. So buckle up. You're in for a hellava ride!"
– J. Michael Major, author of *One Man's Castle*.

Iced, a John Wads Crime Novella, book 1 . . . "Jerry Peterson's new thriller is a thrill-a-minute ride down a slippery slope of suspense and shootouts. Engaging characters, spiffy dialogue, and non-stop action make this one a real winner."
– Michael A. Black, author of *Sleeping Dragons*, a Mack Bolan Executioner novel

A James Early Christmas and *The Santa Train*, Christmas short story collections . . . "These stories are charming, heart-warming, and well-written. It's rare today to see stories that unabashedly champion simple generosity and good will, but Jerry Peterson does both successfully, all the while keeping you entertained with his gentle humor. This should definitely go under your tree this season."
– Libby Hellmann, author of *Nice Girl Does Noir*, a collection of short stories

A James Early Christmas – Book 2, a Christmas short story collection . . . "What brings these Christmas tales to life is the compassion of their protagonist and their vivid sense of time and place. James Early's human warmth tempers the winter landscape of the Kansas plains in the years after World War II. A fine collection."
– Michael Hinden, co-author with Betsy Draine of the Nora Barnes and Toby Sandler mysteries

RUBBED OUT

a John Wads Crime Novella
book 2

Chapter 1

JOHN WADKOWSKI stood scribbling, transferring the gallonage numbers from the gas pumps onto his evening inventory when a pump behind him clicked off.

"Hey, fella," a voice called out.

Wads kept at his recording of numbers, this most routine of his night manager chores.

"Hey, you, Mister Kwik Trip."

Wads swivelled around.

There a stranger at the store's second line of pumps held the nozzle in his truck's filler pipe, his truck a gleaming black Lincoln pickup. "You wouldn't happen to know this area, would you?"

Wads tapped the lead point of his pencil on his inventory sheet. "Grew up here."

"I'm thinking of buying the Pedersen farm. You know the place?"

"Yeah."

A woman in leathers at the next island screwed down the gas cap on her Harley and motored away into the night. The stranger watched her. "She's slim, not the Harley type. Sure wouldn't mind rubbing up against her chassis." After the rumble of the hog faded, he glanced back to Wads. "The Pedersen farm, is it any good?"

"A question first, why are you asking?"

"I'm not from around here you may have guessed." The man squeezed the trigger, pumping another nickel of high test into his truck's tank, to bring his purchase up to an even twenty-five dollars.

He had an easy look about him, a Tom Selleck mustache, gray slacks, a tan zip-up jacket, and tan cowboy boots with walking heels. Wads leaned around to check the heels. He aimed his pencil at the man's ball cap, a Cubs cap. "Illinois?"

"Mundelein." The stranger closed the flapper door on his truck's filler pipe. "I fly for Southwest Airlines. Got me some spare bucks, so I'm looking for a getaway place."

"To get away from Chicago?"

"Yup."

"The Pedersen farm could be it, but let me warn you, it's not much of a farm."

"Why's that?"

"Too many hills and a gawd-awful lot of woods."

"Hey, I'm a deer hunter. That works for me." He sidled along to the back of his truck, his mitt out to shake hands. "Name's Chrisco, Monte Chrisco."

Wads came over and clapped onto the hand. "Don't tell me, the Count."

"Some people call me that. I wish they wouldn't."

"John Wadkowski. Most people call me Wads, and I don't mind it."

"Wads, huh? Maybe I could buy you a beer when you get off. Maybe we can talk some more."

"No beer. Muscle Milk's my drink."

"Strange drink in the state where Leinenkugel's king, but that's all right. Where?"

"The Library."

Chrisco tilted his head.

Wads caught the look of puzzlement. "That's a bar downtown."

"I'll find it then. What time?"

"I check outta here at midnight. Make it five after if you've really got a thirst."

"Twelve-oh-five it is."

Chrisco got in his truck. As he closed the door, Wads hiked off for the front door of the convenience store that he had run on the nightshift for the past year, the store at the edge of Jamestown.

Wads reached for the grab bar, to pull the door open. Behind him tires screeched, then came the sound of metal striking metal. He whipped around in time to see a light pole arcing down over the hood and roof of a black Lincoln pickup.

Chapter 2

WADS RIPPED OPEN the driver's door as the power fizzed out of the front and side air bags. A dazed Monte Chrisco laid there in the seat, his head hard against the headrest, blood dribbling from his nose. He shifted an eye toward Wads. "Wha happen?"

Wads grubbed out a handkerchief. He packed it around Chrisco's nose. "Looks like you busted your beak. You all right?"

"This the way you treat people from Illinois, throw light poles in front of them?"

"We've got an ordinance against light-pole throwing."

Chrisco put his hand on the handkerchief. He pulled it away and squinted at the bloody cloth before he tamped it back under and around his nose. "Musta sprung a leak."

"Sure did, pard. If you think you can stand, I'll help you get out."

The sound of sirens moving at a high speed came up the street, a fire department crash truck the first to wheel into the Kwik Trip, all its emergency lights flashing, followed by an ambulance and a city patrol car. The JFD's second bailed out of the fire truck's shotgun seat. He grabbed his tool kit and trotted over to Wads. "How's the driver? He hurt bad?"

"Broken nose I'd say. Other than that, the damage is all to the truck and the pole."

"That's certain." The fireman took out a small flashlight. He pushed in to Chrisco, Chrisco still in the truck, but now with his legs over the side of the seat, his feet resting on the running board. "Sir, if you don't mind, I'm going to check you over."

"Do whad you have da do."

The fireman lifted Chrisco's right eyelid. He shot the beam of his light in. "You lose control here, blackout maybe?"

"Nod that I can 'member."

He moved the light to Chrisco's other eye. "What do you think happened?"

"Steering wheel jerked in my han', then blam."

"My paramedic's here. I'm going to give you over to him. He'll take you up to the ER and have the docs do a stem to stern exam, just to be on the safe side. That all right with you?"

"Yeah, sure."

The fireman stepped aside where he conferred with the paramedic from the ambulance.

The paramedic then stepped in. "Mister, they call me Shots. I'm gonna take your blood pressure."

The patrolman left his cruiser with clipboard in hand and came to Wads. "Looks like we've got us an accident here. That the way you see it?"

"Pretty much."

"It's on your driveway and not on the street or city property, so I don't see any reason to write this guy up for what happened, do you?"

"Nope."

"Of course, he did cream that light pole, but that belongs to Alliant, not the city."

"He'll probably want an accident report for his insurance company, don'tcha think?"

"I suppose. Okay, here's what I'll do. I'll sketch the scene and do the measurements, but, Wads, then I'm outta here. I'm on overtime as it is, and I wanna get the hell home. Oh, I called Dot to get out here with her tow truck."

Wags slapped the patrolman on the back. "You're a good man, Charlie. Get a coffee on the house before you leave."

The patrolman touched an index finger to his eyebrow in salute as he walked away.

Another set of flashing lights rolled into the Kwik Trip and up to Wads, a rollback hauler with the name Dot's You-Wreck-It-We-Tow-It Service painted on the door.

Dorothy 'Dot' Kranz leaned her elbow out the window and blew a ring of cigar smoke over Wads's head. "My man, I thank you for the bidness. My first tow job in three days."

Wads gave a nod toward the Lincoln. "The hood and roof are bashed in, but the truck may drive."

"Hey, don't you tell the owner. I want my fee." Kranz swung her door open and slid down, her coveralls pressed and her work boots shined. "Any idea why the truck ended up the way it did?"

Wads shook his head.

"Driver drunk?"

"I didn't smell any alcohol, and he says he didn't black out. I see a front tire's flat. Maybe it blew and that did it."

Kranz and Wads watched the paramedic, Eddie Shotzheimer, walk Chrisco to the ambulance, she flicking ashes from her Swisher Sweet. "I'd say this fella looks like he can afford anything I wanna put on his bill."

"He's probably got Triple-A."

"That would be a crimper if Triple-A had called me, but Charlie did, so I can charge any diddle-darn thing I want. Called out at night like this, that's gonna be at least double overtime, triple if I can stretch it to past midnight."

"Dot, you are a robber."

"Hey, don't tell my sister the insurance adjuster."

Wads made a pulling-the-zipper motion across his lips.

She gave a wave to the patrolman reading a measurement off his steel tape. "Charlie, is it all right for me to get that crippled beast outta here?"

"You gonna lift that light pole off the truck?"

"Hell, no."

"Then you'll have to wait on Alliant."

"You call them?"

"Sure did."

A fifth vehicle rolled in, an Alliant Power truck and trailer, the truck's emergency lights flashing. It stopped to the street side of Wads and Kranz. "Wads," the driver called through his rolled-down passenger window, "got room for one more at your party?"

"Sure, it's your light pole."

"I'll tape off the busted wires so you won't get lit up if you touch one, how's that?"

Wads waved an okay.

"Dot, gimme a hand gettin' that big stick outta your way?"

Kranz chewed on her cigar as she jacked up an eyebrow. "I'm a pro-fessional. You gonna pay me?"

"Now, Punky, don't be an old crab."

She blasted smoke from her nostrils. "No pay, no play."

"Well, I'm lucky tonight. I've got The Claw." The utility man eased his truck and trailer up beside the Lincoln. He swung out of the cab like a Simian and up on the back of his truck's bed. There he settled at a control pedestal where he worked a joy stick and a speed controller that lifted an articulated grabber up and over the light pole. He lowered the grabber–the claw–around the pole at its midpoint, clamped the claw tight, and lifted the pole away from the Lincoln and over onto the power company's trailer. He waved to Kranz. "Okay, Punky, the wreck's yours."

After the utility man locked down The Claw, he hopped off and went over to the concrete pad to which the pole had been bolted, to tape off the electrical wires. While he worked, Kranz wheeled her hauler around and backed it in toward the Lincoln.

She left the cab for a panel of controls on the side of her rollback. There she rolled the hauler's bed back and the tail down to the pavement, then spooled out her winch cable. She looped the cable around the tow hooks under the rear of the Lincoln, and, when she had the hook-up secure, began winching the Lincoln back toward her hauler's bed.

The front of the Lincoln swung.

Kranz saw it and let off on her winch. She snorted cigar smoke in Wads's direction. "Need a little help here, buddy boy."

Wads parked his knuckles on his hips. "I'm a professional. You gonna pay me?"

"Fun-ney. Next winter when you skid your truck in a ditch, I'm not gonna pull you out."

"All right, what do you want?"

"Get in that Lincoln. Straighten the front wheels and hold them straight while I winch this sucker up on the bed. You think you can do that?"

Wads shot a thumb in the air.

He climbed into the cab, did as he was instructed, and Kranz winched the Lincoln back and up onto the rollback. She raised the rear of the bed until she could roll the bed back in place against the cab and lock it down.

Wads came around, and there stood Kranz by the front of the Lincoln, running a hand over the flat tire. She beckoned to him. "Come take a look at this."

He did, then cast a sideward stare at Kranz.

She put the beam of her Mag-Lite on the sidewall, on a puncture hole. "Look to you like a bullet did that?"

Chapter 3

BARB LARSON, wearing her trademark bartender's outfit of a black mini-skirt and orange tube-top, set a bottle of Muscle Milk in front of Wads. "Hear you had some excitement at the store."

"Nothing out of the ordinary." He twisted the top off the Muscle Milk—strawberry flavored—and chugged a gulp.

"Someone knocks over a light pole? Shots fired? That's not out of the ordinary?"

"Shots? Oh, right, Eddie came by."

"Smart mouth. Shots like bang, bang."

"Well, maybe just one bang."

Larson wiped down the bar in front of Wads. "So it's true. Is there a contract out on you again?"

"There's no contract."

"How do you know?"

Wads leaned forward until his nose touched Larson's. "I don't. Someone blew out a tire on a customer's pickup. Where do you get this stuff?"

"I listen to the police radio."

The door opened. Wads glanced up in the mirror over the backbar, at the image of two men coming in—one, Monte Chrisco, a bandage over the bridge of his nose, the other, Eddie Shotzheimer in his ambulance crew blues.

Larson waved to them. "Shotzy, who you got there?"

"The injured from out at Wads's store."

"Good, now I can get all the dirt. Wads is here."

Wads gazed at Shotzheimer in the mirror. When Shotzheimer tipped a hand to him, Wads gestured to a booth. Shotzheimer nodded and guided Chrisco off, Wads coming behind them with his Muscle Milk.

The paramedic slid onto a bench seat. "Wads, this fella insisted he had a date with you. Something going on here?"

"Not what you think."

"Anyway, he shouldn't be driving, so I brought him."

Chrisco rubbed at a spot on the table. "In the ambulance."

"Lights and siren?"

Shotzheimer chuckled. "Just lights. Didn't want to get the drunks down here in the bar district agitated."

Chrisco looked up from his job of despotting the table top. "Do you know all they give you at your E.R. is Ginger Ale? After what happened at your store, I really need that beer."

Wads fired two fingers into the air. "Barb, a Fat Tire for the wounded and a Spotted Cow for Shots."

"Comin' up."

"Thanks." Wads stared into the eyes of Chrisco. "Barb thinks somebody's got a contract out on me, but I haven't offended anyone recently. You?"

"Haven't had time. I'm new in your town."

"Well, it wasn't a drive-by, and Charlie canvassed all the houses within a block and no one heard any gunfire."

"Who's Charlie?"

"The city cop."

"Oh. It was a detective who interviewed me at the E.R."

"What'd you tell him?"

"What I told you."

Larson swooped in with the two beers on a tray. She touched Wads's shoulder. "Get any juicy stuff yet?"

"I don't think there's any to be got."

She wedged herself in on Wads's bench seat. "You don't mind if I listen, do you?"

"Don't you have customers to take care of?"

"Just you." She gave him an air kiss. "It's a slow night."

Chrisco took a long pull on his beer, then rolled the half-empty bottle between his hands. "Wads, about this farm I'm interested in–"

Larson perked up. "Farm? What farm?"

Wads nudged her elbow. "The Pedersen place. The Count, here, wants to get away from Chicago."

"The Pedersen farm is haunted."

"What?"

Larson brought out her order pad and proceeded to doodle on it. "Back when I was a kid–the farm had been abandoned for some time back then–we'd see strange lights in the house. One night, on a double-dog-dare-you my friends and I had to go in and something jumped at us, and we ran the heck out of there, screaming."

Chrisco stopped rolling his bottle. "A ghost?"

"I don't know, but we never went back to find out."

"Wads, what do you think?"

"This is the first I've ever heard."

"If it's true, I might be able to do something with that. Ghost tourism, it's big. A haunted farm, huh?" He turned his hands palms up, doing a gimme motion with his fingers. "Come walk the place with me when the sun's up. Let's see what's out there."

Wads stared into his nearly empty bottle of Muscle Milk, silent.

Shotzheimer leaned in. "Wads, I know one of the guys with 'Ghost Hunters.' I can call him, maybe get him to film an episode here. It could make Jimmytown famous."

Wads raised his gaze. He peered at Larson beside him. "Am I getting myself sucked into something here?"

Chapter 4

SHOTZHEIMER JACKED himself forward, his forearms resting on the front seatback of Wads's Silverado dually. "I called Wilferd this morning."

"And?" Wads asked as he kept his eyes forward.

"He's on a shoot in Atchison, Kansas, you know, the most haunted little city in America? Says he'll fly in next week to scout the location."

"You must have fed him some line."

"Just told him what Barb told us."

"Uh-huh."

"From here, he'll go over to Lake Geneva to check out a couple mansions where three of Chicago's richest killed themselves back during the Depression. It's said their spirits still walk their boat docks. Then he's heard the tale of Big Foot in Walworth County. If we had Big Foot here, we'd really have something."

"Do you believe any of this stuff?"

"Well, no. It's only important that Wilferd does and shoots an episode here."

Wads slowed for the turn onto the drive that led to the farm's buildings and the house, Chrisco in the passenger seat, his elbow out the side window and his focus on what laid ahead. He flicked a finger at the house, the roof sagging like a swaybacked horse. "Shabbier than what the pictures at the real estate office show."

Wads peered at the thing, wondering if it should even be called a house. "Tell you what I'd do if I bought this place. I'd insure it high and pray for a fire."

Shotzheimer slapped Wads's shoulder. "Not before Wilferd gets here."

"Count, this is your show. Where do you want to start?"

Chrisco massaged his chin. "Let's assume for the moment that the house is haunted. Why disturb whatever might be there if your friend here's got a ghost hunter coming?"

"So?"

"So let's drive around the acreage and see if we really do have some good deer hunting here."

Wads tapped the screen in his truck's dash, and a Google search page came up. He tapped on 'Favorites', then 'DNR' and scrolled down the new page that opened. He stopped on 'Deer inventory' and tapped on 'Wappello County.' "Just what I thought."

Chrisco leaned over for a better look at the screen. "What's that?"

"The spring inventory shows a herd of twenty-eight deer running these hills. Biggest concentration of deer in the county is right here."

"Hey, I can like that."

Wads came up on an old lane behind the barn. He dropped the truck into low and wheeled around a rut and onto the lane that headed toward the back reaches of the farm. Again he tapped on his screen. This time he brought up a Google Earth aerial view of the farm. Wads waggled his fingers at the screen. "See here? You've got a couple good-sized ponds on the property. You could have ducks and geese here."

"Turkeys?"

Shotzheimer pointed out Chrisco's window. "Seek and ye shall find. Ask and it shall be given unto you."

A tom, a hen, and a half-dozen poults stalked through a meadow, feasting on grasshoppers.

Chrisco shook his head. "This place is a sanctuary for all of nature."

"And ghosts." Shotzheimer grinned at him in the mirror.

Chrisco leaned into the screen for another look. "Have I got a baby ski hill there?"

"You've got lots of hills here, there, and everywhere."

"But this one looks to have some size. How close can you get us?"

Wads stopped the truck. "No closer than this. We've got a fence ahead."

"So let's walk there." Chrisco threw open the passenger door and hiked off.

Wads and Shotzheimer slid off their high seats, closed their doors behind them, and hustled to catch up to Chrisco already at the fence, studying how best to get over it.

"Four strands of barb wire." Wads put his foot on the second strand. He took hold of the third and pulled up, creating a gap. "You don't climb this one. You go through it."

Chrisco and Shotzheimer hunkered down and scuttled their way to the other side, then Shotzheimer held the gap open for Wads.

Chrisco stuffed his hands in his back pockets as he went on. "Any mining around these hills? Gold, silver?"

Wads tromped down on a bull thistle. He twisted on the ball of his foot, crushing the weed at its base. "Gravel, sand."

"Think I've got some here?"

"Here and all around here. We've got more gravel and sand in this part of the county than we have high-grade farm dirt."

Chrisco stopped. He did a slow three-sixty, to take it all in. Shotzheimer stayed with him, but Wads went on and, in an instant and a yelp, dropped from sight.

Chapter 5

WADS LAID CRUMPLED in a gloom . . . of what? Or, more pressing, where?

He struggled, lifting himself onto an elbow. There he did his darnedest to make his eyes focus. But what light Wads sensed was meager and frizzled out in, by his guess, maybe a dozen feet. It was as if he were in the center of a dim, very dim spotlight, the edges of the light frayed.

Wads ratchetted his head around, then up.

Yes, there was a point of light up there.

Did I fall down the rabbit hole? If I did, where's the damn rabbit? Where's Alice?

He brushed at a smattering of debris on the front of his shirt, brushed the debris away—soil and shreds of sod. Around him laid more debris—clods of dirt, some stones that he could see, and a broken tree root.

"Shots? Chrisco?"

Only silence, except for a faint echo from somewhere. Off to the side?

"Shots!"

The light overhead dimmed.

From a form silhouetted by the light came what Wads hoped for. A voice.

"Wads?"

"Shots?"

"Wads, where the hell are you?"

"I don't know. In a hole? If it's a hole, it's a big hole. And deep."

"How deep?"

"Can't tell."

"You all right?"

"Can't be sure. Can't get up."

"All right, here's the paramedic in me. I want you to check your limbs."

"Limbs?"

"Your arms. Your legs. You're looking for broken bones."

Wads ran his free hand over his arm on which he had propped himself. Nothing.

With a monstrous effort, he horsed himself up and onto his butt. He worked a hand down one leg. Seems okay, but the other–

Wads touched the ankle and winced.

"Well?" came Shotzheimer's voice.

"Ankle's bad."

"Whaddayah think?"

"Busted, maybe."

"Oh, jees."

"Can you get me out?"

"I can call the sheriff's department on my cell. They can get their rescue unit out here, but these guys are volunteers. It may take them an hour, an hour and a half."

"Shots, in the back of my truck I've got a cattle rope."

"What?"

"I said I've got a cattle rope."

"Where?"

"Back of my truck."

"We can use that. I can rig a sling in the rope, and the Count and I, we can pull you up."

"Bring my Wagan."

"Wagon? You got a Radio Flyer in the back of your truck, too?"

"No, Wagan–w-a-g-a-n."

"Whatzat?"

"One honkin' big flashlight. Two million candlepower."

Schotzheimer whistled. "That'll sure light up whatever's down there."

"That's my idea."

"All right, I'm on it. Don't you go anywhere."

The light came up full as Shotzheimer pulled away from the top of the hole.

Wads gazed around. Don't go anywhere? Where can I go? God, if my ankle's busted, I'm gonna be in a hospital and no paycheck. I need my paycheck. "Chrisco?"

A new form blotted out a portion of the light. "I'm here."

"Chrisco, you on Obamacare?"

"What'd you say?"

"Are you on Obamacare?"

"Why?"

"Listen, are you on Obamacare?"

"No."

"Company's insurance?"

"Yeah."

"Pretty good?"
"My union says so."
"I'm on Obamacare."
"So?"
"My policy, it's got this steep deductible. A hospital stay will break me."
"Why do you think you'll be in a hospital?"
"My ankle, it's busted, maybe worse."
"Maybe you'd like to talk about something else."
"Like what?"
"Like the hole you're in. It's too big to have been made by some animal, right? Could it be an old well?"
"You don't normally dig wells on hills. No, seems too big for that. And there's no water down here that I can feel."
"I see."
"It's dry. Smells musty. Ooo, just caught a whiff of something I can't identify. Stinky."
"Could you be a cave?"
"Maybe. There are caves around here."
"But here?"
"Seems I remember my dad talking about a cave on this place. I was a little kid at the time, so I don't remember much. I probably hadn't read Tom Sawyer yet or I would have gone exploring."
"A cave? A haunted house? Lots of deer and turkeys? I'm liking this place more and more."
Wads shifted himself onto one ham. "I'm sure the bank wants to get rid of it. They've had to foreclose on it a handful of times. You see Shots?"
"He's pounding up the hill."

"Good. I gotta pee. I sure don't want to do it in my pants."

"He's here."

The light brightened and dimmed again.

"Wads?"

"Shots?"

"Here comes your big flashlight."

Wads squinted up at a form descending toward him. It came down in his lap. He worked the rope free and gave a yank on it. "Got the light."

"I'm gonna pull the rope up now, tie a sling into the end of it, and drop it back down to you, all right?"

"All right." Wads, while he waited, pressed the button on the handle of his flashlight, and the Wagan shot out a searchlight-strength beam that slapped into a rock wall some distance away. He moved the beam to the side and picked up a grayish formation that rose from the floor upward maybe four feet, he estimated. A stalagmite.

He played the light up, up from where the stalagmite ended in a blunted tip to a stalactite descending from the ceiling, its tip appearing to be dagger sharp.

"Whaddayah see, Wads?"

"This is a cave, all right." He moved the light to the side and down, illuminating more formations, several with color—ruby and emerald, most just variations of gray. The beam came to rest on a rubble of rock. "Off to my left, it looks like the roof has collapsed."

"How close?"

"Twenty yards could be."

"What else?"

Wads swivelled and shot the beam in the opposite direction. "Looks like a passageway to my right. Goes some distance, I can't tell how far. Some downgrade. Floor looks to be pretty smooth that way."

Wads heard something behind him, something sliding. He swivelled further and brought the light over his shoulder. "Shots, what do you call a gang of snakes?"

"Here comes the rope. A gang of snakes? A nest. If they're rattlesnakes, they're called a rhumba. Learned that playing Scrabble at the fire station."

"Get me out of here, Shots. I've got a rhumba behind me."

"The hell you say."

"I do say."

"How close?"

"Six feet. On a shelf of rock." Something touched Wads lap, and he bounced.

A loop of rope.

"You got the rope yet?"

"Yeah."

"No more talking. Get the sling under your arms. You pull on the rope when you're ready, and the Count and I will do the rest."

Wads worked the sling over his arms and head until it came across his back, the knotted end in front of him. He yanked on the knot while behind him something buzzed.

Wads felt the sling tighten under his arms and across his back, felt himself being dragged upward, felt something strike the heel of his boot while he concentrated on the light above, on the light coming closer, the light inviting escape.

The rope raked to the side, hauling down dirt and rock. Wads felt himself drop with the mess, in free fall, until the sling snapped tight, cutting under his arms. He felt a band of pain and himself swinging in the semi-darkness, as if he were a pendulum in a grandfather's clock.

"You all right, Wads?"

"What happened?"

"Rope ripped the hole open. It's hard against a tree root now. We're gonna pull you up again."

"Make it fast. I can hear those snakes."

Still swinging, Wads again felt himself being inched upward, rising toward the light, rising, rising enough that he at long last could get a hand on the tree root over which the rope raked. He glanced down. "Shots, stop. Don't pull me out. Tie off the rope and get me a stick, a long stick."

"What's going on?"

"A rattlesnake's bit my boot. He can't let go. I've gotta knock him off."

Chapter 6

WADS HOBBLED into the Kwik Trip on crutches, an aircast wrapped around and over his left foot and ankle.

Cindy, his tall night clerk, stared at the aircast. "What happened to you?"

"Well, I fell through the roof of this cave—"

"Right."

"—into this rhumba of rattlesnakes."

"Rhumba?"

"Den."

"Uh-huh."

"You don't believe me."

"Boss, you can tell me you fell out of bed. You really can."

"But I didn't."

"Whatever." She glanced up at a CCTV screen, one of six showing the convenience store's pump area. On the screen, a teenager with a three-gallon gas can dismounted his BMX bike. "Boss, he's here again."

Wads twisted around to get a better look at the screen. "Oh, our little gas thief. It's time we learned him a lesson."

The kid, in low-hanging jeans, tennies, and a flat-billed ball cap, the bill twisted to the side, popped the cap off his gas can. He stuck the nozzle from pump eight in and squeezed the trigger. Wads waggled a finger at the control board. "Cut his pump."

Cindy tapped pump eight's STOP button. Together, she and Wads watched the boy pull the nozzle out of the can, watched him stick it back in and jerk the trigger, and jerk it again. The boy slammed the nozzle into the pump and, irritation clouding his face, jockeyed to the next pump where he proceeded to take down that pump's nozzle and insert it into his gas can.

Wads, leaning on his crutches, folded his arms before him. "Give him a tenth, then cut him off again."

Cindy watched the numbers flash up to zero-zero-point-one-zero on the meter for pump ten and tapped the STOP button.

She chuckled and Wads snorted at a repeat of the action from pump eight–the jerking on the trigger, the slamming the nozzle into the pump, the moving on to the next pump. This time the boy added something new. He kicked the pump before he took down the nozzle.

Wads rubbed his hands together. "Oh, I just love this. Give him another tenth and cut him off."

Cindy again watched the digits flash up on the meter, this time for pump twelve. At the magic zero-zero-point-one-zero, she touched the STOP button.

The kid stared at the nozzle, a dribble of gasoline burbling from it. He jerked the trigger. When nothing happened, he hammered the heel of his hand into the pump's CALL FOR HELP button. "Yer gawddamn gas pumps don't work, you know that?"

Wads leaned over to the squawk box. "Thank you, sir. We've been having a problem. I'll be right out." He picked up a screwdriver from beside the speaker and started away. "Cindy, when I look up into the camera, you turn the pump on."

She gave a thumbs-up, and he went on outside, swinging along on his crutches to the gas island where the teenager stewed. "Hey, there."

"Hey, there yerself. What kinda crummy place is this yer runnin' here?"

"Be at peace, son, these things happen." Wads hunkered down in front of pump twelve. He stuck the end of his screwdriver into the slot beneath the nozzle and rattled the end around, his face scrunching up as he faked working. He glanced up at the camera, and the pump motor whirred. "There we go."

The boy reached for the nozzle, but Wads stopped him. "Why don't you let me fill your can for you? Least I can do, and you deserve a little extra service for all the trouble you've had. That's what we pride ourselves on here at Kwik Trip, providing extra service."

Wads stuck the nozzle in the plastic gas can and squeezed the trigger. "Three gallons?"

"Yeah." The boy nodded at Wads's aircast. "What happened, old man?"

"Fell through the roof of a cave."

"You jerkin' me?"

Wads gave him the raised-eyebrow thing before he turned his attention to the digits rising on the pump's meter. When the gallonage neared three, he backed off on the trigger, slowing the flow of gasoline. "Why don't I stop it on an even ten dollars so I don't have to make change for you?"

The youth didn't answer.

Wads clicked off the pump at ten and slipped the nozzle back into its holder in the pump's housing while the boy slapped the cap on his gas can.

Wads polished his hand on his trouser leg. "That'll be ten dollars."

The kid came up, and, in a blur of movement, jabbed his elbow hard into Wads's chest, throwing him back onto the pavement. "I never pay, old man."

The kid scooped up his gas can. As he did, Wads rolled to his side and swung a crutch for all he was worth at the kid's near ankle, unending him.

The teen fell into his bike.

Wads scuttled to him and, with his other crutch, pinned the boy there.

The boy kicked at Wads.

Wads dodged the flashing Adidas. He horsed himself around and came down hard on the boy's back. Wads sat on him, the boy jerking and kicking.

He dope-slapped the kid. "You kick, I slap, and I can keep it up all night. Can you?"

A police car raced in, its blue lights pulsing and siren winding down. The cruiser stopped beside the jumble of bodies, one kicking at the other, the other slapping back. The patrolman, Charley D'Haze, leaned out his window. "You having fun there, Wads?"

Chapter 7

WADS TWISTED the cap off a bottle of Joe—"water with a work ethic" said the label—and threw back a slug. He wiped his lips on his sleeve. "I'm getting too old to be wrestling with teenagers."

Cindy looked up from her counting of the cash in the drawer. "That's certain."

"Cind, you make me feel so good."

"No, really. You're almost as old as my dad, and he's really old."

"How old is that?"

"Thirty-eight."

Wads slapped his forehead.

"Boss, I've been trying all night to work up to telling you something."

Wads peered at his bottle of Joe.

"I'm going to have to quit."

"Because of that ruckus out front?"

"No, that was fun. It was. It's just that—"

"Spit it out, girl."

"—well, I want to work with hair."

"You're kidding me, right? You want to be a stylist, you with your long, straight unstyled hair?"

"No, a barber. I've enrolled in barber school."

Wads shook his head. "And where do you do this barber schooling?"

"Milwaukee, at the tech college. I can come home and work on the weekends if you want. The money would help."

"Cutting hair. You're not gonna wanna practice on me, are you?"

The tall night clerk laughed. "You, boss, you I want to practice shaving with a straight razor."

"Sure, you do. Cind, the antiquers call those things cutthroats and for good reason. No thankee, Bullwinkle."

THE MILLER CLOCK over the back mirror at The Library chimed the quarter hour–a quarter past midnight.

Wads ignored it. He sat at the bar, staring into his bottle of Muscle Milk. "Can you believe it, Cindy wants to go to barber school? Where am I gonna get someone as good as her to take her place?"

Barb Larson opened a cranberry Sierra Mist for herself and sipped from it. "Advertise, my friend, advertise."

"I've already emailed the newspaper, and Cindy whomped together a help-wanted poster she put in the front window."

"There you go." Larson planted a warm kiss on Wads's forehead, startling him.

"What's that for?"

"A little comfort. You looked so glum, chum."

Monte Chrisco came bustling in through the front door and clamped an arm around Wads's shoulders. "Buddy boy, I want you to see this." He poked his iPhone in front of Wads and, with his thumb, tapped his way through a series of icons, bringing up the result of a Google search.

"Yeah?"

"Well, read it."

Wads put his gaze to wandering across the lines and down the screen. "I'll be darned."

Chrisco turned the screen to Larson. "The cave on the Pedersen place I want to buy, there was a stage in it and lights and electricity. They broadcast a polka show from there in Nineteen Forty-Eight, The Three Fat Dutchman, whoever they were, Frankie Yankovic, and Lawrence Welk. Isn't this something? Frankie Yankovic, was that Weird Al's grandfather?"

Larson pulled a file folder from beneath the bar. "Find anything else?"

"That's all that was on the net."

"You didn't happen to think to try the newspaper, did you, Ace?"

"Barkeep, all newspapers are on the net."

"Not the old ones."

"Whaddaya mean?"

"Just out of curiosity, and because I think you're bug crazy, I went to our Carnegie this afternoon. I rolled my way through some of the microfilms of the Jimmytown Herald's Nineteen Thirties editions, and guess what?" She took a sheet from the folder. She played with it for a long moment before she laid it in front of Chrisco. He and Wads read down.

Chrisco tapped a paragraph as he at the same moment elbowed Wads. "Would you look at this? They not only had a stage in the cave, they had a speakeasy. Barkeep, this calls for a beer and another Muscle Milk for Wads and whatever for you. A Pink Lady?"

"Thanks, but no thanks. I'm on duty." Larson brought out a Fat Tire and a Muscle Milk. She jacked off the caps and set the Fat Tire in front of Chrisco and the Muscle Milk in front of Wads.

Chrisco held his bottle out in a toast. "My friends, this is getting better and better."

Wads clicked his bottle against Chrisco's. Not Larson. Instead she watched them, watched them as they hauled down a couple swallows.

Chrisco raked his fingers up through his forelock. "A speakeasy, can you imagine? I wonder if the law ever tried to shut it down."

Larson brought out a second paper. "In the time I had left, all I could find was this editorial." She handed it to Chrisco. "The editor rips the sheriff for ignoring The Classy Lassie Subterranean as the joint apparently was called. The sheriff, it seems, was a cousin of the man who owned the farm."

"Collusion, huh?"

"Would seem to be."

"I love it. Wads, look here at this date, October Nineteen Thirty-One, the twelfth. Now you know there's got to be more. How about you join me in the morning at your fair city's hall of books that Andrew built?"

Chapter 8

WADS SWUNG ALONG on his crutches into the Jamestown Carnegie Free Library and up to the checkout counter. There he gave a foolish grin to the librarian, Melinda Grodivant by her name tag.

She gazed down at his aircast.

Wads shrugged. "Yes, I know we're supposed to start rehearsing tomorrow for the library's fundraiser. Dancing With The Jimmytown Stars, it's not gonna work."

"I know that's what you want me to think, but I also know you can buy one of those wrap things at any drugstore. You're faking this, aren't you?"

"Shots was there when this happened."

"When what happened?"

"When I fell through the roof of this cave."

"Oh, Wads, I'd believe you if you said you slipped in the shower, but not this."

"I've got a copy of Shots's report."

Grodivant threw up her hands. "He lies for you."

Wads pulled a wrinkled paper from his back pocket. He smoothed it on the counter before the librarian.

"What's this?"

"A note from the E.R. doctor."

She read it, tilting her head as she did. "A sprain, really? Nothing strenuous for two weeks, she says. Wads, how about we go for the sympathy vote and do the routine we've got choreographed with you in a wheelchair."

"Are you serious?"

"I'm not going to let you poop out on this."

"A wheelchair?"

She nodded.

He leaned more heavily on his crutches. "Tomorrow?"

"Two o'clock."

"I guess." Wads scribbled the time on the back of the doctor's note that he then stuffed back into his back pocket. "I want to look through some old microfilms of The Herald. Where do you keep them?"

"You're the second to ask today."

"The other a guy in a Cubs cap and cowboy boots?"

"You know him?"

"Monte Chrisco."

"Pardon?"

"Never mind. The microfilms?"

"Back in the reference department. You remember where that is, don't you?" She gave him the cool eye.

Wads pushed off. He made his way toward the back of the library, toward the collections of encyclopedias, maps, census reports, directories of several long-defunct local telephone companies, and catalogued collections of letters and service records from the county's warriors who had gone off to first the Civil War and every war thereafter. A copy of his record was there and his letters that he had written to his father from Iraq and Afghanistan, all given by his father to the library. Wads had considered donating his dad's end of the correspondence—he had saved all those letters from home about the changing seasons that he was missing on the farm, his old girlfriend getting married, the death of his dog from cancer—but he just hadn't been able to part with them. Someday, maybe.

He glanced to the side as he approached the reference desk and saw Chrisco in the AV room, hunched over a screen. He diverted and tapped the Chicagoan's chair with his crutch.

Chrisco leaned back and rubbed his eyes. "I've been reading for an hour, and I haven't found a thing. I'm in Nineteen Thirty-Two."

"What do you want me to do?"

Chrisco flicked his fingers at a microfilm reader across the table. "I've set you up there with everything from Nineteen Thirty-Three. I need coffee. You wouldn't happen to have brought some?"

"There's a machine in the basement."

While Wads hobbled around to the other reader, Chrisco stretched. He got up. "Guess I'll go to the basement. You want a cup?"

Wads pointed his crutch at the hefty librarian parked behind the reference desk. "Name's Helen Bonebrake. She's the library's enforcer. Rule number one, no food or drink outside the basement lunchroom. Violate that rule and you'll find her name applies."

"Oh, come on."

"Bring a cup of coffee up here and see what happens."

Chrisco appraised the woman. "She does outweigh me."

He left, and Wads settled in to the task at hand. He clicked the light on on his reader and cranked away at the take-up reel. Pages of The Herald crawled across the reader's screen, pages of each week's issue starting with January Fourth. He scanned down the front page and inside to the first week's courthouse report, then the second week's in the next issue. He stopped on two names under "Marriage licences issued"–Kazmierz Wadkowski and Malgorzata Sobczak.

His grandparents.

Wads reeled on, looking for the wedding story and found it a month of issues later, only two paragraphs listing his great grandparents' names, others in the families who were there, the church where the wedding was held–St. Stanislaus Catholic– and a note that the Wadkowskis would be living on a farm on Sawicki Road, the farm where Wads had been born.

He wound through the rest of that reel and loaded in another.

Chrisco came back into the AV room, reeking of coffee. "Before you say anything, the machine didn't drop a cup, so I got splashed."

"Sorry to hear that."

"Turned out okay. The library director was very apologetic. He put in his own dollar and banged on the side of the machine twice. You gotta do that to get a cup to drop, he said. A cup did and it filled. The stuff's not half bad." Chrisco sat and commenced cranking on his reel of microfilm. "Come across anything interesting?"

"A story about my grandparents' wedding and another about the price of milk in the spring of 'Thirty-Three. Did you know farmers in this county were getting only eighty-six cents for a hundred pounds of milk?"

"How would I? I'm a city guy."

"For the love of Mike, man, the dairy farmers here and elsewhere were going broke."

"So?"

Wads spooled on only to stop on a front page story headlined LOCAL FARMER KILLED IN MILK STRIKE. "Ohmigod."

"What?"

"We had milk strikes in Wisconsin in 'Thirty-Three. We read about them in history class, but never this."

"Never what?"

"Listen to this from the May Twenty-third issue of our paper, 'Boogumil Wadkowski of Centron Road shot by creamery guard Charles Gilcrest while dumping kerosene in the Jamestown Creamery's bulk milk tank.' Boogumil, that had to be my grandfather's brother. He was listed in the wedding story."

Chrisco leaned away from his reader. "Gilcrest did you say? Charles Gilcrest?"

"Uh-huh."

"That name's on the Pedersen deed, on the list of past owners."

Wads scanned further down the front page. "Hey, here's a story about a preacher leading a group of his parishioners picketing the entrance to Charles Gilcrest's farm and the speakeasy in the cave. 'The Reverend Jedediah Barzak, pastor of the Dry Creek Primitive Baptist Church, and two dozen of his followers last week turned cars away trying to enter the farm.'"

Wads cranked the microfilm forward to the next week's issue. "Look at this."

"Whaddaya got now?"

"BARTZ WOMAN LEADS CARRIE NATION RAID ON GILCREST SALOON . . . 'Miss Oldriska Moravek of Bartz and a group of women from the Saint Procopius Catholic Church of the same community wielding hatchets and crowbars on Saturday destroyed much of the interior of the tavern-in-a-cave on the Charles Gilcrest farm, according to a complaint filed with the sheriff's department by Mr. Gilcrest in which he denied that his establishment served anything stronger than near beer.'"

Chrisco broke up, laughing. "Free publicity, man. I love it."

"I guess."

"If I had a bar, I'd pay somebody to do a Carrie Nation on it."

Wads scanned the rest of the story, then cranked on to the next week's issue. "Small story here. Remember Oldriska Moravek and her hatchet?"

"Yeah."

"Her family reports her missing and her sister, Ivona."

"So?"

"That's it. Nothing more." Again, Wads cranked on. "Hell and damn."

"Now what? I find nothing and you find all the good stuff?"

"Chrisco, that rubble I saw in the cave. Here's the story, CAVE ENTRANCE DYNAMITED."

Chapter 9

WADS, SWEATING, his frustration growing, worked a wallpaper brush across the back of an oversized static-cling sign he'd been trying to position in his store's front window, squeegeeing out the air bubbles that kept sneaking under the graphics and message proclaiming that Kwik Trip now carried steaks and chicken–everything for your next cookout. While he scrubbed and pulled the plastic back and scrubbed some more, someone on a motorcycle rolled in across the tarmac and parked in front of his window. Wads eyed the driver as he readjusted the plastic one last time, this time to get the sign square, the driver in leathers taking off her helmet and shaking out her hair.

She swung off the saddle and came inside, to the counter, to Cindy the night clerk stocking the cigarette case. "Sign in the window says you need help. I'd like to apply."

Tall Cindy thumbed to Wads still scrubbing at the plastic that had now afixed itself to the glass as if by super glue, out of plumb, bubbles and all.

The biker glanced at him, then strode over. "Are you the boss?" "Of the night shift." Wads mopped his sleeve across his forehead before he laid his brush aside, on the Twinkies display.

"The sign says you need a clerk."

"I do. You ever work in a convenience store?"

"No, but I've worked at Target."

"Worked? Like in the past tense?"

"Uh-huh."

"How long?"

"Four months."

"What happened?"

The biker sucked in a breath. "It's this way, my supervisor couldn't keep his hands to himself."

"Did you report him?"

"I did, but the store manager didn't do anything. So it was either kick my supervisor in the balls and be fired or quit. I chose to quit."

"Are you always this blunt?"

"I like to think of it as being upfront."

Wads gave a jerk of his head toward the cash register. "Mind if we go over so Cindy can listen in? She holds the job right now."

"Fine by me."

As he and the biker strolled along, she stripped off her gloves. Wads inched up an eyebrow at the ocelot tattoo on the back of her hand. "I'm curious."

"About this?" She brushed her gem-studded fingernails over the tat.

"No, about why you want the night shift."

"I'm a student at Otterbein."

"Oh, our Methodist college."

"The one."

"So what's you major?"

"Primary education."

"Ah-ha, want to be a teacher."

"Like my mom."

They came up to Cindy flattening a stack of empty cigarette cartons.

"Cindy, I'd like you to meet—what's your name?"

"Catherine. Catherine Chow. Everyone calls me Cat."

A glimmer came into Wads's eye. "Cat Chow, aisle three."

Chow's eyebrows knit together into a solid line as she stared up at him. "Is that your idea of humor?"

"I thought it was pretty good."

"Then I guess I'm not interested in your job."

"Wait a minute. Back up. Forget I said Cat Chow, aisle three. I think you could work out here. You're a tough little broad."

"Got your foot in your mouth again?"

Wads, bewildered, looked to Cindy, his hand trembling. "Won't you help me out here?"

"I'm rather enjoying this."

"Cindy—"

The tall night clerk came around the counter. She took Chow by the elbow and guided her to the door. "Catherine, I like you. Why don't you wait by your ride a couple minutes so the boss and I can talk?"

Chow, a head and a half shorter than Cindy, went on out and parked her butt on her Kawasaki.

Cindy swivelled back to Wads. "I sure can see why no woman wants to marry you. You've got a mouth that's just hard to take."

Wads shrugged. "I thought I was just making a joke."

"You thought? No, you didn't think. I like that young woman. You see that tattoo, those fingernails, the bike she drives? No customer's gonna fool with her, and that's what you need when I'm no longer here."

"But she's so short. She can't see from one aisle over the displays to the next."

"Boss, this store's covered by more cameras than the Big Brother house. All she's gotta do is watch the monitors."

Wads leaned back against the counter. He braced himself with the heels of hands. "So you think I should hire her?"

"I watched you. That's what you were intending to do before you let off with that stupid crack about cat food in aisle three."

A gas customer, wearing a fishing vest and a hat with a dozen flies hooked around the crown, pushed his way into the store. He slapped a twenty-dollar bill on the counter, next to Wads's hand. "Set me up on pump three, wouldja, bud?"

Wads reached back to the panel of pump controls and tapped in the command for pump three to shut off when it hit twenty dollars of product. He tapped the START button. "Anything else for you, sir?"

"A coffee and a hot sub sandwich."

"What kind?"

"How about turkey on rye with Swiss and brown mustard?"

"We're on it."

The man moseyed back out to the pumps where his pickup and a trailer with a bass boat on it waited.

Cindy diverted to the deli counter. There she broke out the makings for the sandwich. "Back to Catherine, what are you going to do?"

"If I hire her, will you train her?"

"Of course. If I let you do it, you're likely to rip off with some wiseacre remark that'll get her mad again."

Wads blew out a lungful of air as he went to the front door. He leaned out and beckoned to Chow.

She came in, one eyebrow raised, suspicion tiptoeing around her face.

Wads clapped his hands together. "The job, it's yours if you want it."

"Is there a catch here?"

"No. But you do have to fill out an application. The company requires it."

"Are you going to be calling my old boss at Target?"

"Look, I don't care what happened there. It's past. It's done. Kwik Trip will run a background check on you. Again, it's S.O.P., but if you don't have a criminal record, I can tell you now you're in."

"I don't."

"Excellent. When do you want to start?"

"I could be here tomorrow night."

Behind Wads, Cindy shot a mustard-covered thumb into the air.

Chapter 10

WADS, IN HIS OFFICE, wagged a product sheet at a cadaverously thin man chatting with Cindy, the night clerk. The man, in shirt sleeves pushed above his elbows and necktie pulled loose, waved a zippered leather case at Wads, then went back to visiting with Cindy.

Wads horsed himself up. He went to the door. "Howard?"

"Yeah?"

"If you can rip yourself away, I'm the one who called you, remember?"

Howard Zigman, a detective with the Wappello County Sheriff's Department, drummed his fingertips on the counter. "Is he back on coffee again? He seems a bit agitated."

"It's not caffeine. He just doesn't like change. See, I'm leaving."

"You are?"

"Barber school."

"So this—" Zigman gestured at Chow hunkered down in a near aisle, the night clerk-in-training slashing open a carton of Campbell's soup with a case knife.

"She's the next me."

"When's your last night?"

"Friday."

Zigman pushed back from the counter. "Maybe we can get something up before you leave. Right now I better go back and talk with the troll." He helped himself to a stubby bottle of Cherry Coke from one of the store's coolers as he made his way to the back, to Wads's office. "Evening."

Wads jerked a plastic chair out from the wall for Zigman. "It is that, plus some."

The detective settled in. He threw one leg over the other before he twisted the cap off his drink. Zigman held the bottle up. "Here's to a little relief from the heat. The A.C.'s dead in my cruiser." He rubbed the cold Coke across his forehead. "So Cindy's leaving."

"She told you?"

"Uh-huh. Tell me about the new girl."

"Catherine 'Cat' Chow. And don't make any fancy remarks about her name or she's likely to do a number on you with her box cutter."

"She zing you?"

"Yup."

"What else?"

"In the fall, Miss Chow'll be a sophomore at Otterbein. Wants to be a teacher. Did you see that black Kawasaki parked at the side of the store?"

Zigman winked at the comment, then threw back a hefty swallow of Coke.

Wads fiddled with his product sheet. "That's hers. I don't know a lot about motorcycles, so I googled it. A ZX-12R sport bike, top-of-the line and screaming fast."

"So her dad's got—" Zigman rubbed the tips of his fingers together.

"I haven't asked. What have you got for me?"

Zigman unzipped his case. "You never knew you had a great uncle, huh?"

"Dad never mentioned him, and, as for my grandfather saying he had a brother, if he did I don't remember. I was a kid when he died."

Zigman pulled out a kraft envelope brittle from age. From it, he extracted two pages, the typed copy several shades from new. He placed the pages on Wads's desk. "Boogumil Wadkowski, age forty-seven at the time he was shot, the weapon a Remington twelve-gauge. Wife, Edyta, deceased previous by two years. No record of children. A brother, Kazmierz Wadkowski, claimed the body. Kazmierz, that would be your grandfather, right?"

"That's him."

"Charles Gilcrest was charged with manslaughter, but you know that. You'll find the deputy's report is pretty darn thorough, remarkable for Nineteen Thirty-Three."

Wads turned the pages to himself. He moved his finger down from paragraph to paragraph as he scanned them. "There's nothing here about the disposition."

"That would be in the court record. You didn't ask me for that. It took me a half a day just to find this." Zigman took a pull on his Coke. "You think this might have something to do with the dynamiting on Gilcrest's farm?"

"Maybe. Or maybe the preacher who was picketing the place did it."

"Would you be interested in the deputy's report on that?"

Wads glanced up, surprise lighting his face.

Zigman brought out a second brittle envelope. He shook out a single sheet of lined paper, the notes on it handwritten in pencil. "I couldn't find a formal report. May have been lost over the years."

Wads took the sheet and read down it to the bottom. He turned the sheet over, but found the second side blank. "Not much here, is there?"

"It rained that night and that whole area was a cow pasture, so any footprints or tire tracks were obliterated. Just some soggy cigarette butts and a stick of unexploded TNT."

"Wonder where that came from?"

"Back then, you could buy dynamite at any hardware store. Farmers would get a stick or two to blow a tree stump out of the ground. Nobody kept records."

Wads waved a hand over the page. "Nothing here says the deputy interviewed anybody."

"Nope."

"Would you have interviewed somebody?"

"Of course. But then that's my job. I'd want to know where the preacher was and your grandfather and maybe Missus Gilcrest. She might have had it in for her husband. You know these Polacks."

Monte Chrisco hustled in through Wads's office door. He slapped a hand on Zigman's shoulder. "Sorry to interrupt, buddy, but this is important."

Wads, as he popped up, poked a finger at Zigman. "Zig, this is the Count."

Zigman, too, came up. He reached for Chrisco's paw and gave it a quick pump. "You the guy who got his tire shot out here the other night?"

"The same."

"How's the nose?"

Chrisco felt around the bandage. "Still hurts. I must look like a bandit with these black eyes."

"The bruises should start to fade in a couple days."

"That's what the E.R. doc told me."

Wads picked up a Bic pen. He jiggled it in his hand. "Count, Howard Zigman is a friend and a detective in the sheriff's department."

"John Law, that's a good friend to have. Wads, I came in to tell you I bought the Pedersen farm today. Tomorrow, an excavator with an endloader and a backhoe is gonna open up the cave. Want to come out and explore it with me, maybe bring your friend?"

Chapter 11

CHRISCO, WADS, AND ZIGMAN, looking like the three Musketeers in modern dress, strolled up to the cave's entrance, Chrisco twirling a walking stick as a swordsman might a rapier while a backhoe raked the last of the rocks away.

Chrisco rapped his stick on the backhoe's fender.

The man at the controls glanced over. He cut the machine's engine, then peered down at Chrisco, grinning. "Got 'er done, bosso."

"Mister Jiggs, you do good work."

"Aw, waddn't too bad a job."

"How far did you have to dig to get to where the roof was solid?"

"Fifteen, maybe twenty feet." Jiggs pulled off his cap. After he mopped his hair back with the back of his hand, he motioned ahead. "With the opening I've got for you now, you could drive a Jeep in there. That's something, ain't it?"

"You'll send me your bill?"

"Right-o, bosso. By the way, your snake wrangler's in there."

Chrisco waved and went on with Wads and Zigman at his side, Wads hobbling on his crutches.

"Snake wrangler?" Zigman asked.

"When Wads fell through the roof of the cave, he came down among a den of rattlers, so I hired a guy to round 'em up and take 'em away. He milks them for their venom."

"The snake wrangler, that wouldn't happen to be Marley Mudd?"

"You know him?"

Zigman stopped. He kicked a stone away. "Old Marley, I've had to arrest him a couple times."

"For what?"

"Trespass. When he goes hunting diamondbacks and timber rattlers, he doesn't much care whose property he's on. Wads, you ever meet him?"

Wads shook his head. "'Fraid so. I prefer to keep my distance, a lot of distance."

"Yes, he is a mite whiffy."

"Rancid's more like it. Maybe that draws the snakes to him." Wads moved out on his crutches into the cave's entrance. He ducked beneath the ledge of rock that marked the beginning of the roof. Zigman and Chrisco did the same as they came along behind. They brought out their flashlights and turned them on.

Wads snapped on his Wagan as well. He swung the monster light's beam to the side where it illuminated some kind of odd contraption, rusting and dust covered, a pipe going from it up through the rock of the roof. He went over and swiped a hand across a plate on the side of the machine, revealing a name. "Just what I thought, a generator made by Fairbanks Morse. Count, you said this place had its own electricity."

Chrisco swept his light over the machine and out along an insulated wire that ran away from the generator along the side of the cave. His light reflected off something. "Oh, my, that's a safety globe for a light there. Wonder if we got this thing running if we'd have lights all the way back into the cave?"

"I just wonder how far back this cave goes."

"That's what we've come to find out." Chrisco moved on, playing his light over the cave's floor, much of it flat and appearing to slope ever so slightly downward as it went. He led Wads and Zigman around a bend, into an area illuminated by a series of gas lanterns.

To the side worked someone with a long pole, the pole with a hook on the end of it.

"Mister Mudd?"

"Shut yer yap. I'm busy." The snake wrangler worked the hook under the belly of a lethargic rattlesnake on a ledge. He lifted the snake away, the snake dangling over the hook as if it were asleep. Mudd inched around. When he caught sight of Zigman, he thrust the snake at him. "Here you sumbitch."

Zigman whipped his Glock out of his belt holster and triggered off a shot, deafening in the enclosed space. The shot blasted the snake's head away.

Mudd's eyes filled with anger. "What ta hell you do dat for? He's no good to me dead. Big snake like dat, he had a lot of poison in him. He was worth money, maaann."

Zigman leveled his pistol at Mudd. "You're damn lucky I didn't shoot you."

"Sumbitch."

Chrisco waved his hands. "Whoa now here, whoa now. Detective, I hired Mister Mudd to do some work for me. Let's let him keep at it. We'll just skirt around him and go on, is that all right?"

Zigman holstered his weapon. He sidestepped away and down the cave, all the time keeping his eyes fixed on Mudd and his hand on the grip of his pistol.

Wads followed.

Chrisco took a step to the side as well. "Mister Mudd, I'm sorry about this."

"Sorry don't feed the bulldog. Keep that sumbitch away from me."

"You've got my word." Chrisco scuttled further to the side and away into the dark in an effort to catch up with Wads and Zigman. He found them some distance on, sitting on the edge of a stage in an area of the cave that, as the three played their flashlights around, bulged out into a kind of ballroom.

Wads patted the stage. "This must be where they broadcast from. The musicians would have performed up here."

He swung his light around behind him. "Back there appears to be a bar. Want to check it out?"

"I could use a drink what with wild Quick Draw McGraw here. Good God, man."

Zigman stuck his flashlight beneath his chin as a kid might intent on scaring others. "I don't much care for snakes nor snake wranglers."

Wads slapped Zigman in the middle of the back. "Come on, the bar calleth."

The trio wandered on, aiming the beams of their flashlights here and there, picking up safety light globes, a broken chair and table, and side passages that appeared to lead deeper into the cave.

Wads went around behind the bar. There he swept the beam of his Wagan along the shelf beneath it. "Bingo."

He brought up a single liquor bottle. Wads brushed the dust from the label. "Canadian Rye. This is bootleg stuff, eighty years old if it's a day. Corked and sealed."

Chrisco swiped the bottle away. He broke the wax seal and with his thumbs worked the cork out of the top of the bottle. Done, he threw back a slug. After a large swallow, Chrisco grinned. "Damn good stuff." He held the bottle out to Wads.

"No thanks. I'm a reformed drunk. And don't bother offering it to Quick Draw. He's drinks only Baptist gin."

Chrisco settled on his elbows on the bar. He cradled the bottle in his hands and studied it. "Do you suppose the county would give me a liquor license?"

"Why would you want one?"

"Think of the possibilities. Wads, I could rig this place out like a gangster saloon. I could even bring in Al Capone's car. See, I know the guy who owns it, and he owes me a favor. You want to be a partner in this with me?"

Zigman aimed his light at his watch. "You two can dream all you want. I have to get back to Jimmytown. I'm up to testify in a robbery trial."

Wads came around the bar on his crutches. "You don't go anywhere without me, remember? I drove."

Chrisco stared at his bottle. "Well, I guess we're done here then."

He, too, swung away, and the three made their way back to where Mudd was collecting his gas lanterns, a gunnysack off to the side, tied shut and its contents churning.

Mudd glanced up at Chrisco. "Wanna guess how many I got?"

"A couple dozen?"

"Thirty-seven. Woulda been thirty-eight if ya hadn'tta brought dat killer down here. Might still be a couple more snakes around, up in the rocks, that won't return to the nest 'til night. You want me to come back and see?"

"Absolutely."

Wads shot the beam of his Wagan back along the ledge that had been home to the vipers. He stopped when something white appeared in the light. "Is that what I think it is?"

Zigman stepped forward. He aimed his flashlight's beam in as well, all the time squinting at the object. "Great Aunt Fanny, looks like a skull."

He reached into the crevice for it, but Mudd slapped his arm away. "You got yerself a death wish or sumpin'? You don't know as I mighta missed a rattler back in there."

Mudd elbowed Zigman out of the way and went fishing with his pole. He worked the hook end around until it slipped into an eye socket. He then reeled the pole back until he had the skull on the lip of the ledge.

Zigman again reached for it, and again Mudd batted his hand away.

A short, well-fed rattlesnake rolled itself out from the skull through the gap beneath the lower jaw.

Chapter 12

WADS ON A CANE and a walking cast, Cindy the night clerk, Chow the night clerk in training, and Zigman, each toting a Kwik Trip green bag, boiled in through the front door of The Library, the bar pulsing with polka music blasting from the jukebox and women dancing, the air rich with the aroma of beer.

Wads cupped a hand to his mouth. "Hey, barkeep, pretty durn loud in here, isn't it?"

Barb Larson hiked up a thumb. "It's a party! You want in?"

"Nope, we're gonna have a party of our own!" He aimed his cane at a booth. "My usual, a Baptist gin, and two diet Sprites."

"Big drinkers." Larson grinned and went about pulling up bottles for the order.

Wads wove his way through the dancers, Cindy, Chow, and Zigman tight behind him, to the booth, the table still wet from being wiped down. He gestured for his compatriots to slide in. Before each did, they plunked their bags on the table. From his, Wads took out a box and from it extracted a cake with a single candle in the center. He made a show of setting the cake in front of Cindy.

She came up on her elbows, the better to read the message piped on in white frosting over chocolate: *Hey, barber-to-be, we'll miss you.* That followed by three hearts.

Cindy gazed up at Wads. "Boss, this is so sweet."

"Darn right it is. Double chocolate. Your mom told me it's your favorite."

Her eyes narrowed. "You didn't make it, did you?"

Wads's smile drained away. "Oh, what a cut."

"You did make it?"

"Of course. With bourbon."

"You're kidding."

"No, chocolate-chocolate bourbon cake. Cracker Barrel makes theirs with Coca-Cola. I use bourbon, Wild Turkey Rare Breed Barrel Proof Bourbon."

Cindy pitched up an eyebrow at Chow. "You just can't be sure when he's telling the truth or giving you a fish tale."

"All right, it's Old Wads Private Reserve. I made it in my bathroom and aged it in a plastic jug."

"That's more like the truth."

Wads gave up. He sat down. As he did, Larson pushed in with a tray of drinks. She passed a Muscle Milk–strawberry flavored–to Wads and a Coke to Zigman. "That means the Sprites are for you," she said as she set two glasses still fizzing with carbonation in front of the girls. "As long as you don't ask for beer or something stronger, I don't have to card you."

She nudged Wads with her hip. "So what's your party about?"

The polka music played out, and the dancers rambled off to their tables.

Wads rubbed at his ear. "I thought for a while I was gonna go deaf."

"They paid me to turn the volume up. So what about your party?"

"Cindy here, she's leaving the employ of our grand and glorious Kwik Trip store to go to barber school." He handed Cindy a Bic lighter and gestured at the candle. "Make us some fire, kiddo."

She flicked up a flame and put it to the candle's wick. "You're not going to sing, are you?"

"The only song I know is 'There's a Tavern in the Town,' and Barb won't let me sing it."

The wick caught. It flamed up and, after a moment, settled down to a steady burn, a steady burn that erupted into a shower of sparks, followed by a whistle and three thumps—small balls of fire arching up toward the ceiling—a mini Roman candle.

Cindy, Chow, and Zigman yanked back, and Larson ran for a fire extinguisher. The dancers, across the room, jerked away from their beers and assorted drinks and gasped.

Wads took it all in, grinning like Alice's Cheshire.

When Larson galloped back with the fire extinguisher, he stuck out his hand to block her. "Show's over."

"You are one crazy—"

"If I were crazy, I would have made a real Roman candle."

"You knew what you were doing?"

"I didn't take chemistry in high school for nothing."

The dancers eased back to their steins and wine and martini glasses, and their conversations while Cindy and Chow shook the shock out of their frames.

Zigman, though, studied the singe marks on the ceiling.

Wads went to rustling around in his green bag. He unearthed a small package wrapped in the Jamestown Herald's sports page and held the package out to Cindy. "Time for some serious gift giving."

Chow and Zigman dipped into their green bags as well. They, too, brought out small packages that they pushed in front of Cindy.

She clasped her hands together. "You people shouldn't have."

Zigman gestured at his.

"All right, I'll open yours first." Cindy ripped away scotch-taped red tissue paper to reveal a hand mirror. She peered at herself in the glass, her face distorted. "Wavy glass in the mirror? You expect me to hand this to a customer and ask how's your haircut look? Where'd you get this, at a carnival fun house?"

Zigman snickered, covering his snorts with his hand.

Chow, with the tips of her fingers, inched her package—a small gift bag—closer.

Cindy reached in. She withdrew something wrapped in white tissue, peeled the paper away, and held up a troll doll, its brush of hair tied up with a red ribbon.

Chow beckoned for the doll. "I want you to know the hair, this is a real barber's neck brush. I got it at a beauty supply store. And this doll that Mom and I put together with the brush, that was one of hers when she was a kid."

Cindy took the troll back. "I love it, thank you." She picked up Wads's package. "So now I have to open this one, huh?"

"It's the last of the first round."

"You mean there's more?"

"Oh, yes."

Cindy tentatively, cautiously tore at the newspaper wrapping until out came a hand clippers. "What, no plug?"

"It's not electric, sweetie. This is what the old-time barbers used to cut hair. It's an antique."

"Like you?"

Wads clutched at his heart. "You've injured me again."

He, Chow, and Zigman once more dipped into their bags for a second set of packages, Wads's package again wrapped in newspaper.

Cindy selected that first. As she held it up, she gazed at Wads. "Do I dare?"

"It's something you can use. Honest."

She tugged at the paper until it fell away, revealing an electric clippers this time, with three changeable blades. "You spent a lot for this, didn't you?"

Wads shrugged. "Keep it clean, my barber says, and it'll last you a lifetime."

Cindy went at Zigman's package next. Out from the wrapping came a mug and brush. Zigman handed over a round bar of shaving soap. "This goes with it, for when you have to shave someone. With a straight razor."

"Gawd, I will have to do that, won't I?" Cindy turned to the last, again a gift bag. She reached in and extracted a handful of cloth, hair clippers-patterned.

Chow waved her gem-studded fingernails at it. "Open it all the way."

Cindy gave the cloth a sharp snap, and it transformed into a barber's smock. "I love this."

"The fabric's special. It sheds hair. Also in the bag, there's a matching chair cloth."

"Did you make this?"

"Sure, give me a sewing machine and I'm little Miss Kitty Homemaker."

Cindy folded the smock, and, as she put it back in the gift bag, she gazed around the table. "I cannot tell you how much this means to me."

Wads waved his hands. "Now don't tear up on us."

She sniffled and reached for a tissue. "I can't help it. Anyway, when Mister Zigman let it slip that you were planning something for my last night, I had to get something for each of you."

Zigman wagged a finger. "You didn't have to."

"I wanted to. I really did." From her green bag, she brought out an envelope. This she handed it to Zigman. "A Kwik Trip gift card. It's good for a case of Cherry Coke."

To Chow, she placed a small box in her hands. "Inside is hair chalk. I caught you looking at it when we got it in the other night, so I know you're dying to try it."

After some moments, she looked at Wads and held out a soft package. "My mom and dad went to Czechoslovakia last summer, to see their grandparents, my great grandparents. While they were there, they found a t-shirt they said was perfect for you."

Wads opened the package, grimacing as he did. He let the paper drop to the floor and held up the gift, a blaze orange t-shirt with a mug of beer printed on it, foam sliding down the side, and the words *Dej mi hubicku za pivo*. Wads stared at Cindy. "What's this say?"

"I don't know. I don't read Czech. My Grandma Jakubec could translate it for us if she were here."

"And the beer?"

"Well, that's the joke. My parents know you don't drink. Go ahead, put it on."

Wads pulled the tee over his head and down over his shirt and did a pirouette, to show off the tee.

One of the women at a side table whistled.

Wads swivelled to her.

She pointed to his tee. "Do you mean what it says there?"

"I guess."

She and her cluster rose from their tables as if they were one and hustled over. The first to Wads planted a wet kiss on his mouth.

Shocked, he pulled back. "What's this about?"

"Your t-shirt. It says 'Give me kiss for beer.'"
"What?"
"It says 'Give me kiss for beer.'" She put her hand over her heart. "I'm Czech. We're all Czech. This is my bachelorette party. I'm getting married tomorrow. Come on, where's my beer? Make it root beer. I'm the only one at my party not drinking."

WADS FLOPPED in a captain's chair, his elbow on an arm, his hand cupped to the side of his face. "I'm done. Those Czech girls, I can't polka anymore."

Zigman sipped from his Coke. "It's all because of your t-shirt."

"Thank you, Cindy Jakubec."

Larson rang a bell over the bar. "Closing in ten minutes. Last call!"

Wads gave a weary wave.

Across the way, the bachelorette party broke up. Most moved toward the door, several unsteadily, hanging onto one another, but the honored guest who had kissed Wads came over. She kissed him again, this time on top of his head. "Thanks for the beer and the dance and the dance after that. You dance pretty good for someone in a walking cast."

She slid a piece of paper torn from a napkin onto the table and dawdled over it. "See you at my wedding? You and your friend are invited."

"Sorry, I sleep days."

"Don't tell me you're Dracula."

"No, I work the night shift at the Kwik Trip."

"I'll look for you sometime. I gas up my Harley there."

"Oh?"

She lifted her fingers away from the paper and left.

Zigman peered at the slip. He reached for it and turned it over. "My friend, she's left you a telephone number. Want to guess whose it is?"

"Not really." Wads rubbed his face, his five-o'clock shadow getting onto seven sandpapering the skin of his hands.

Zigman pulled a paper of his own from his inside jacket pocket, the paper folded. "Remember that skull we found in the cave?"

Wads continued to rub his face.

"Got the report from the state crime lab. The part of the skull that was missing, they think it may have been shot away."

Wads stopped rubbing. "Shot away? The person was killed? Murdered?"

"Maybe."

"What else?"

"The techs extracted DNA from a tooth, all X chromosomes."

"Female?"

Zigman popped a finger pistol at him.

"Age?"

"The wear on the teeth suggest maybe about thirty or so."

"They come up with an idea of when she died?"

"Uh-huh."

"Well?"

"By doing some fancy carbon dating, the techs estimate she's been in the cave for eighty, maybe ninety years, give or take a decade."

Wads knitted the fingers of his hands together behind his head. He pulled down and two vertebra gave off cracking sounds. "Wonder where the rest of her bones are?"

"I wonder how she came to be in that cave in the first place."

Chapter 13

WADS HUSTLED IN from the stockroom toting a case of motor oil. He dropped it in the miscellaneous aisle where Chow was straightening the merchandise in the disposable diapers section. Wads looked over at her as he slashed open the case. "I've been meaning to say you've really done something wild with your hair chalk tonight."

She swivelled to him, the overhead lights glinting off her contact lenses. "It's my Norse mythology look." Chow drew her fingertips along the jagged white highlights that led from her temples to well behind her ears.

Wads pulled out four quarts of Quaker State thirty-weight and shoved them in on the bottom shelf. "Ah-ha, Thor. Lightning bolts."

Two people in leathers sauntered into the store, both with helmets tucked under their arms—a man and a woman—the woman gazing around, as if she were looking for someone. When she came into Wads's and Chow's aisle, she stopped and pointed at Wads on his knees. "Oh, there you are."

He glanced up, his hands grasping another four quarts. "It's me, all right. And who are you?"

"Don't you remember?"

"Afraid not." Wads shoved the oil onto the shelf and the last four quarts as well, emptying the case.

"Last month? My bachelorette party? *Dej mi hubicku za pivo?*"

"Ohmigod."

"Anna Doskocil. Well, Anna Deleatorre now."

Wads pushed himself up. He swiped his right hand on his jeans before he extended it to the woman.

She took his hand and held it for a long moment before she glanced at her husband. "Wads, this is the man I married, Alejandro Deleatorre. Alex, actually."

"Sir," Wads said as he shook hands with the stoic. "Your wife made me buy her a beer at her bachelorette party."

"She told me the story. I would have done the same had I been you."

"Yeah, well, thanks. So you're both bikers, huh? What do you drive?"

Deleatorre put his arm around Wads's shoulders and drew him around the end cap to the front window of the store. He motioned to the Harleys parked at the closest gas pumps. "That Iron Eight Eighty-Three, that's Anna's. I drive the big hog. The Street Glide Special, that's mine."

Wads whistled. "How much did that set you back?"

"All tricked out, a bit more than thirty-four thou."

"You coulda bought a really good pickup for that."

"I've got a really good pickup and a Lexus LFA."

Anna Deleatorre came up. She slipped her arm through her husband's, smiling, her teeth so even, so stunningly white. "He has all the toys."

A black Lincoln pickup rolled in and across the tarmac to a stop in front of the window. Chrisco bailed out. He hustled inside, waving his hands, beckoning for applause.

Wads, clapping, came away from the biker pair. He gave Chrisco a low five. "Where've you been for the last month?"

"My friend, I'm like you. I have to make a living. I've been flying extra routes for the company, off the books, so I could get the next two weeks to be up here."

"Why so?"

"Haven't you heard?"

"Apparently not."

"I'm gonna pitch your county zoning board for a change. I'm asking for my farm to be zoned commercial so I can open a saloon in my cave. Huh? How about that." He peered over Wads's shoulder to the leathered pair. "Who're they?"

Wads swung back to the bikers. "Anna and Alex Deleatorre."

Chrisco gave them a two-fingered wave. "Hi ya." He touched Wads's shoulder. "How about you come out to my house in the morning. I'll show you my plans."

"You're living at your farm?"

"Well, this is my first night."

"The house is haunted, you've heard, remember?"

"Maybe I'll meet the ghost of whoever died in my cave. Wouldn't that be great?"

Chapter 14

CHRISCO UNROLLED a set of blueprints onto a worktable made from a pair of hollow-core doors, the room bare except for the table, two ladderback chairs, and a pine tree air-freshener hanging from the shade in a window. He set a hammer on one corner of the blueprints and sacks of nails on the other corners, to hold the paper flat. "You know what my biggest problem is?"

Wads sucked up a mouthful of decaf from a styrofoam cup, decaf he'd bought at the Mickey D on his way out. "Ghosts?"

"No. Ghosts, if I have any here, they're an asset, not a problem."

"Did you see any last night? Maybe hear some strange noises?" Wads waggled a hand and made a wavering ooooo sound.

"Some noises, yes."

"Like what?"

"Furniture being dragged around down here."

"Well?"

"But nothing was. Everything was where it was supposed to be here, the front room, the room that's to be my study, and the kitchen. I checked twice in the night and again this morning."

"Strange."

"That it is. But the problem in the cave?"

"Power I suppose."

"No, we'll bring a line in off the two-twenty running along the county road. And I'll have the Fairbanks Morse restored for a backup generator. No, the problem is sewage."

"Pardon?"

"I have to put in toilets and a commercial kitchen with sinks. All the drains are going to be below the level of the opening to the cave, so I can't have a gravity-flow system to get rid of the sewage."

"I see."

"I either have to pump it out to a wastewater system that I'll have to build or each morning have someone come in and suck it up into a honey wagon and haul it away, likely to your city's sewer plant."

"Count, you want to be in the entertainment business, not the wastewater business. Contract with one of the Johnny-on-the-Job guys and have it hauled."

"Yeah, that's probably best." Chrisco swept a hand over the blueprints. "Here you can see where the utilities and the electricals go and where we'll be building walls, but this doesn't give you any idea of what my saloon is gonna look like."

He next unrolled a set of artist's renderings, laid them over the blueprints and tagged down the corners. "We've got a firm of restaurant designers in Chicago, I mean top-notch, expensive as all hell, and here's what we've worked out."

Wads leaned over a pencil drawing bathed in watercolors that showed the entrance to the cave, a neon sign above it proclaiming Bullets Chrisco's Speakeasy.

Chrisco grinned like a baby with gas. "Like the name? Bullets?"

"It's appropriate for what you want to do."

"I'm gonna have three Packard low-rider convertibles built, the four-door Model Nine-oh-Four. Uniformed chauffers will meet our guests at the parking lot and transport them into the cave–into the speakeasy–where they will let them off at our ballroom-slash-saloon."

"No password?"

"Oh, yes, they have to know the password before someone will open the doors at the entrance for the cars."

"You're really going to do this up, aren't you?"

"See here, here, and here." Chrisco tapped a finger on renderings of classic cars inside the cave, along the drive to the saloon. "I'll have automobiles of the era for guests to look at and have their pictures taken in. Nothing cheap. No Model A's. Pierce Arrows, Duesenbergs, cars like that. And see here." His hand stopped on a diorama. "Remember there are two side caves? This will be in the first, a re-creation of the Saint Valentine's Day Massacre, before there was any shooting–Bugs Moran's gang lined up against the wall of the Clark Street Garage, see, being held there at gunpoint by Al Capone's gang, two of them dressed as policemen. Mannequins, but the night we open, they're going to be actors, and we're going to do the massacre. It'll blow everyone's minds."

"And eardrums with all that shooting."

"Hadn't thought about that. Anyway, the bar, back bar, stage, and ballroom areas, everything plush. Nineteen Twenties over-the-top—crystal chandeliers, the most expensive fabrics, the finest woods, leather."

Wads parked his elbows on the table. His hands supported his chin as he gazed at the rendering of the back bar. "You didn't miss anything, did you?"

Chrisco strode over to the side window in his farmhouse's dining room. The window overlooked a ragged garden. He stood there, knuckles on hips, studying a hummingbird helicoptering among a cluster of honeysuckle blossoms. "There is one thing."

He whipped around to Wads and, as he did, the glass behind him exploded.

Chapter 15

CHRISCO DOVE for the floor, glass showering him. Once flat, he cocked an eye toward Wads, also hugging the floor. "What the hell happened?"
"Count, you may be earning your new moniker."
"'Bullets'?"
"Didja hear that pop?"
"Huh-uh."
"Rifle fire. Got a gun?"
"No."
"Stay down then. Got your cell?"
"Yeah."
"Call nine-one-one." Wads rolled toward the kitchen.
"Where you going?"
"Out to recon."
Chrisco dug in his pants pocket for his phone. While he did, Wads came up. He scuttled toward the back door and outside where he stopped at the corner of the house. He peered around the corner, toward where he thought the shot may have come from.
Fifty yards beyond the ragged garden stood a shabby fence near fully engulfed by wild grape vines,

a line of hickory trees and a cornfield beyond that, lots of cover for someone out to kill.

Wads crouched low. He burst around the corner and ran hard for the fence, bailed over it and came down in a burdock patch in tall grass, yelping as burs drove through his clothes and into his skin. Wads forced himself to his knees. He pulled at the burs as he poked his head up only to yank himself down when a shot furrowed the grass inches to his right.

An engine started.

He heard it and again came up, this time like someone who had been swatted across the rear with a two-by-four. Wads raced after the sound of the engine, a motorcycle bellowing away, throwing up a roostertail of dirt from the edge of the cornfield. The bike rocketed through a ditch and bent away up the county road.

Wads, sucking for wind, staggered to a stop where the bike had churned up the soil. He bent down and braced his hands on his knees, his chest heaving. It ached so. *Maybe Cindy's right. Maybe I am an antique.*

A siren bore through his thoughts, a siren coming up the county road fast from the direction opposite the one in which the biker had fled.

WADS SAT on the trunk of Zigman's cruiser, picking burs off his pant legs, while Zigman leaned against the fender, scratching notes on a pad in his leather case.

"So one shot through the window of the house, you think at Chrisco, and one shot at you out here. Wads, I'd say in the last year you've become one popular guy to shoot at."

"Funnyyyy."

"So who do you think would want to kill Chrisco?"

"Kill? Maybe he only wanted to scare him."

"All right, who do you think would want to scare Chrisco?"

Wads pitched the last bur away. "I haven't got idea one."

"We found where the shooter fired from at the house. We didn't find a shell, so he must have policed his brass." Zigman glanced up at Wads. "The distance from the firing point to the house suggests you're right, he used a rifle."

Zigman's radio crackled. He pulled it from his belt holster and pressed the transmit button. "Go ahead."

"Detective?"

"Yeah."

"I found something."

"Well, don't keep me in suspense, Manny."

"It's the bullet. I dug it out of the wall. It's in pretty good shape."

"Caliber?"

"Eyeballing it, I'd say it's either a twenty-two long rifle or a two twenty-three from an AR-Fifteen."

"If I wanted to kill someone, I'd go with the assault rifle."

"I'll be able to tell you for sure when I get the bullet on a scale."

"Yeah, thanks." Zigman jammed his radio back in its holster.

A tech working at a computer in the back of a crime scene van parked next to Zigman's cruiser peered up from what he had been studying on his screen. "Detective, you're gonna want to look at this."

Zigman pushed away from his cruiser. He stepped around to the tech, Wads with him.

The tech ran his finger over an image on the left side of his screen. "This is a picture I took of the biker's tire track. It'd be the rear tire."

Zigman put on his glasses. He leaned in, tilting his head back to better see through his half-moon readers. Zigman motioned with his pen at a ragged line that ran across the image. "What's this?"

"Looks like a tear in the tread. Could have got it off-roading."

"Fresh?"

"Doesn't look that way, but here's what you want to see." The tech tapped the tread image on the right side of his screen. "This is from our database. Your tire matches this one. It's a Michelin Pilot Power Three."

"For what kind of bike?"

"A Kawasaki. Specifically, a Ninja."

Wads pulled Zigman away. "There's got to be a mistake here."

"How so?"

"What I heard boogie out of the cornfield was a Harley. No other bike in the world makes a blatting racket like it."

"I'll give you that. So tell me what else you remember?"

"The engine noise, yes. The color. The bike was black."

"Model?"

Wads pressed at his temples, to force forward what he had seen. "No. No, all I saw was the back end. With all that dirt flying, I don't know what it was."

"How about the driver?"

"Leathers, black like the bike. Nothing distinctive that I can see in my memory."

"No big Harley logo on the back of the jacket?"

"Not that I can remember."

"Helmet or no?"

"A helmet, yeah. It was round. That's not much help, I know."

"So we've got a driver wearing a helmet. That means no hair color." Zigman spread his hands wide. "He could even be bald."

Wads shrugged.

Zigman sucked on his pen. "My friend, all we've got to work with is a bullet and this Michelin tire tread."

Chapter 16

WADS SLURRIED out a glass coffee pot and wiped it dry while Chow placed a new basket of mellow Arabica grounds in the Bunn.

Done, she brushed her hands on a cleaning towel. "I don't know why, as good as that stuff smells, I just can't stand to drink it."

Wads set the pot back in place before he popped the ON button. "Makes me glad you're not a customer. I wouldn't make any money on you."

Zigman came in. He stopped at the front counter and tapped the bell. "Can I get a little service here?"

Wads checked his watch. "Darn little. It's break time for me."

"Well, I didn't come to see you anyway." He beckoned at Chow.

A questioning expression took up residence on her face as she touched a fingertip to her chest.

Zigman nodded.

She strolled up to the counter, tossing the questioning look back at Wads.

Zigman thumbed at the door. "I want to look at the tires on your motorcycle."

"Why?"

"Your boss may have told you someone this morning shot at him and Chrisco, someone on a motorcycle, a Kawasaki Ninja by the tire tread. I'd like to eliminate you from the suspect pool."

"Me, a suspect?"

"Uh-huh."

"Why would I shoot at anyone? I'm a black belt. I don't need gun to hurt someone."

"Cat, you drive a Ninja."

Her eyes narrowed. "Do you have a warrant?"

"No."

"Then go to hell." Chow spun away and marched up to Wads still at the coffee station. "If you're thinking of asking me to cooperate with that storm trooper, you can go to hell, too."

Chapter 17

WADS SAT in the back row, next to a sheriff's deputy the size of a Green Bay Packers center, listening to Chrisco explain his plans to the county zoning board.

Chrisco, standing next to his artist rendering, faced quarter to the audience and more to the board members seated at a long table. He brought his hands together in a prayer tent. "So there you have it. Right now my farm is mostly woods, so you're only getting a dollop of property taxes from it. With what I want to do–a three-million-dollar investment–I'm going to create all kinds of short-term work for local contractors, a dozen permanent jobs–full-time jobs–how many part-time jobs I don't know, and in excess of a hundred-thousand dollars a year in property and other local taxes. Most of that tax income will come to the county and the school district. I'll take questions."

The chair–Wilma Heinzelman, a no-smoking by county ordinance sign on the wall behind her–lit the cigarette in her holder. She took a long drag, then blew the smoke to the side. "Mister Chrisco, this interests us and our planning staff who supports your petition. We're always looking for new tax revenue."

A husky, square-jawed man with a close-cropped beard shot to his feet. "Madam Chairman—"

Heinzelman pulled her granny glasses down on the bridge of her nose and peered over them. "Chair, Reverend Barzak. You know I prefer to be called Chair."

The preacher smoothed the lapels of his suit coat. "Madam Chair—Wilma."

"Yes, Lucian?"

"May I speak?"

She glanced up the table, caught several nods from her colleagues, then down for more before she turned her attention back to Barzak. "Normally, I take questions from my fellow board members first, but this is a public hearing. We were going to get to you, so it might as well be now."

Barzak fired an accusing finger at Chrisco's drawing. "I'm opposed to that."

"Lucian, you're opposed to about everything except Sunday morning church, but you've got the floor." Heinzelman tapped ashes from her cigarette into a used coffee cup. "For now you have."

Barzak swivelled to the audience. He waved for people to stand.

A dozen did, half of them thrusting up hand-printed placards that read 'Down with Demon Booze', 'Defend righteous living, oppose rezoning', 'Praise God and pass the grape juice', 'These lips will never touch liquor, yours shouldn't neither', 'Be sober. Love your Bible', and 'Tread on us and God will strike you dead'.

Heinzelman rapped a gavel once for order, a gavel that had been at the ready next to her coffee cup-slash-ashtray. "Lucian, these all members of your Dry Creek Church?"

"That's right."

"Just wanted to be sure."

"Wilma, you know our prayer house is but hardly a mile from where this heathen Jew—" Barzak wagged his Bible at Chrisco. "—wants to build this den of iniquity."

Heinzelman raised a multi-ringed finger. "Whoa, now. Let's stop this." She rotated her hand to Chrisco. "Sir, are you a heathen Jew?"

Chrisco tugged at his earlobe, grinning. "A mongrel American, ma'am, and a Presbyterian."

The Chair gazed once more at the preacher.

He took that as a signal that the ball was back in his court. "Still, that man wants to build this den of iniquity, this insult to God—"

"It's a tavern, Lucian. I grant you, it's a slicked-up tavern. But it's still a tavern, and may I remind you taverns are legal in Wisconsin, have been since the German beer makers settled Milwaukee, except for the decade and a half of Prohibition."

"And, praise God, those Prohibition years were glorious years. My grandfather, the Reverend Jedediah Barzak who founded my little church as a Temperance church and was its first pastor, he led the attack on the speakeasy in that very cave on the old Pedersen farm, then the Gilcrest farm. When Gilcrest and others, including you in county government at the time, ignored the protests of him and his little band of the faithful, he blew up the cave—"

Wads glanced up, startled out of a paperback he had been perusing.

"—and, by God, Wilma, you may force me to do the same thing if you let this change in zoning go through. Do you want that on your soul? How're you going to explain that to God?"

Heinzelman aimed the hammer end of her gavel at Barzak. "Let me get this right, you're threatening to dynamite Mister Chrisco's business if we let him build it?"

"I'm God's avenging warrior. Liquor is a tool of the devil."

"Are you threatening me, too?"

"Because you own a liquor store? We're talking about it, talking about holding prayer vigils on the public sidewalk in front of your store. We'll pray for your soul, Sister Wilma, right there on the sidewalk every day and every night for as long as it takes."

"To put me out of business?"

"Hallelujah."

Heinzelman leaned back in her chair, her cigarette holder pinched hard between the second and third fingers of her left hand. "Sit down, Reverend. You've been heard."

"But—"

She whipped forward on her elbows. "You've been heard, Reverend. It's time to give someone else a chance to speak."

"But I have more to say."

"You always have more to say, Lucian. Sit down, or I have a deputy in the back of the room who will remove you."

"I'm a citizen and a taxpayer. I have a right to my say." He swung to his followers and raised an encouraging hand.

That brought shouts of "You tell 'em, Preacher!" and "Freedom. Freedom from drink is our gospel!" One woman began singing *Onward Christian Soldiers*.

Heinzelman shot up, banging her gavel for order, and the deputy rushed away from Wads, to the front. He grabbed Barzak in a bear hug and hustled him out of the room. The preacher's followers ran after the deputy, yelling and whacking him with their placards.

After some moments, with half the audience gone and the remainder settling back in their chairs, gabbling among themselves, Heinzelman stopped pounding the table. She set her gavel aside and glowered at those still in the room. "Does anyone else want to speak on the issue before this board?"

Several stared at their shoes. Others mumbled something to their neighbors, but no one stood up.

"All right then, I call for the vote." Heinzelman turned to the board members on her right. "All those in favor of changing the zoning for the old Pedersen farm, now the Chrisco farm, from agriculture to commercial, please raise your hand."

Four of the four did and three to her left as well.

Heinzelman gazed over at the lone dissenter. "Albert?"

Albert Shankmeyer, a bespeckled lawyer, spread his fingers on the tabletop. "I'm a Dry, always have been and always will be. You know that, Wilma."

"I do. And I respect the grace with which you maintain your position. However, I must inform you and the audience that, on a vote of seven to one, your colleagues have approved this change in zoning."

Chapter 18

CHOW SAT at the front counter of the Kwik Trip, sipping a Rockstar blue raspberry and reading the Jamestown Herald. "I see the county is going to let your friend build his bar-in-a-cave."

Wads looked up from running a Bissell sweeper over the carpet at the door to the world outside. "Why am I doing this? This is your job."

"I'm on break. So about your friend."

Wads, finished, parked the sweeper in a cabinet behind the dairy case. He ambled over to the front counter where he leaned on the palm of his hand and gazed out the window to the gas islands slick and glistening in the overhead lights. "Sure is a slow night."

"Rain's always bad for business." Chow turned a page to the editorials.

"It is that. Mind if I ask you a question?"

"You're the boss. You can do anything you want."

Wads glanced at her from the corner of his eye. "Yeah. Anyway, why'd you get so testy with Zigman the other night when he wanted to look at your bike's tires?"

"I don't like police."

"Why?"

"It's genetic."

"Pardon?"

She closed her newspaper. "How much do you know about the history of us Chinese in your country?"

"You mean our country. It's yours, too."

"Is it?" Chow tugged on Wads's sleeve, to get his attention, but he continued to peer outside. "Let me ask you, if my skin was as yellow as my great grandparents' and my eyes as slanty as theirs, if I spoke with their broken English, would this be my country?"

"Of course."

"Boss, no."

Wads made a business of studying a raindrop slithering down the window glass. "Why wouldn't it be? Why shouldn't it be?"

"It should be, but–"

"But what?"

Chow ran a finger around the rim of her drink can, again and a third time. "My great grandparents, they fled here before World War Two, to escape the invading Japanese. The only place safe for them was Chinatown in San Francisco. When they would venture outside, you cannot imagine the abuse they would take from you Americans–you white people. You thought they were Japs because of their color and their eyes. And your police were the worst."

Wads wanted to say don't blame me, I wasn't there, but Chow was on such a roll that she hardly paused for a breath.

Her eyes flashed fire. "During the Korean War, now you knew my great grandparents and their children were Chinese. Skin color, slanty eyes, right? You thought surely they must be communists because they were Chinese, communists out to kill your sons."

"Oh, come on now."

"Boss, you brought this up."

Wads shook his head. "I never guessed I was going to get a lecture."

"You don't know our history because you didn't live it." She spit the words out as if they tasted of gypsum.

Wads wanted for everything to put his arm around Chow's shoulders, to say it's all right, it's past, but he knew it would be wrong to do so, that his touch would be misinterpreted. Instead, he asked, "Your father, was it better for him?"

"Initially, no."

"Why's that?"

"He grew up in the Chinatown slums of Chicago, turned of age during the Vietnam war, had a low number, got drafted. But, when he got his letter, he told me that he knew then that everything would change if he only he survived the next two years."

Wads chuckled. "He must have. You're here."

She chilled him with a stink eye.

"Just trying for a little humor."

"It's not working."

"Okay, your father."

"He came home to the GI Bill, boss. He knew now he could do something no one in his family had done before. He could go to college."

"And did he?"

"Madison, can you believe it, this skinny kid from the slums of Chicago, only a little older than me? UW, then law school. Law, your law that had made life so difficult for us Chinese since the days you shipped us in by the boatload to build the transcontinental railroad. Coolies we were, coolies. Kept in our place by the railroad police, then, when we made it into our Chinatowns, kept in our place by your city police."

"That was then. This is now."

"Is it? Ask my black friends who get pulled over if they dare drive through Maple Bluff at night. That's where the governor's mansion is, the governor for all of us who live in our fair state. All of us. Now there's the joke."

Chapter 19

WADS AND ZIGMAN heard a pump organ wheezing out a hymn as they climbed the stoop of the Dry Creek Primitive Baptist Church, stepping up past clusters of English rose bushes, the blooms perfuming the air with a spicy scent.

Zigman glanced at his ride-along buddy for the day. "'Jesus Calls Us.' We sing it in my church, too . . . Jesus calls us o'er the tumult / Of life's wild and restless sea."

"You want me to harmonize on the bass line?"

"Not necessary. Your voice down there is way too rumbly." The sheriff's detective opened the door and gestured in. "Shall we, Brother Wads?"

"After you, Brother Zig."

With that, Zigman proceeded in and down the aisle, Wads behind him, to the person thumping away at the organ, his back to them. Zigman stopped short of the man and waited for a break in the music, then cleared his throat.

The organist swung around, away from the keyboard and the stops—Reverend Lucian Barzak, smiling. "Is there something I can do for you?"

"Can we talk?"

He motioned to the first pew, hard-backed, hard-seated oak.

Zigman sat down, but Wads stayed standing. He leaned on the back of the pew.

Zigman placed his leather case in his lap. "Know this guy who's with me?"

"We've not met, but I've seen him here and there." The preacher stuck his hand out to Wads. "I'm Reverend Barzak, but you probably know that."

Wads tested the grip of the preacher's hand and estimated it to be just shy of that of a wildcat trap. "John Wadkowski."

"Yes, you were at the zoning board meeting the other day, trying to read a dime novel when I was speaking as I recall."

"You got me."

Barzak turned his attention to Zigman. "I didn't catch your name."

"Howard Zigman."

"What do you do, Mister Zigman?"

"I work for the sheriff's department."

"Duty?"

"Detective."

"Your being here, does this have something to do with that monster-sized deputy dragging me out of the hearing room?"

"Somewhat." Zigman unzipped his leather case. He opened it to a transcript that he laid on the bench seat where Barzak could see it from his place at the organ but not read it. "Wads told me you said your grandfather dynamited the Gilcrest cave back in Nineteen Thirty-three. I find that strange."

"Why?"

"It's not in the deputy's report at the time—I looked it up—nor in the newspaper story about the explosion. Wads happened to come across that while looking for something else. Why do you suppose that is, Reverend?"

"It's simple."

"How so?"

"My grandfather swore to Daddy and me that he never told anybody except us, and then only us when he was dying."

"Why is that?"

"He said he didn't want to go to jail and have to abandon his flock."

Zigman tugged at the knee of one trouser leg, to take the tension off the fabric. "I read the transcript of the hearing. You said you'd blow up the cave if the county let Mister Chrisco proceed."

"Detective, I'd never do that. I'm a man of God."

"Then why'd you say it?"

"To keep the spirits of my flock high."

Zigman tucked the transcript back in his case. "You said it for domestic consumption, so to speak."

"So to speak, yes."

Zigman peered up at Wads. "We're done here, wouldn't you say?"

Wads gave a shrug of his shoulder.

Zigman zipped his case shut and shuffled to his feet. He started up the aisle with Wads beside him, only to turn back. "Reverend, one last thing."

Barzak, who had already been resetting the stops for the next hymn he wanted to rehearse, swivelled around on his stool.

"When they opened up the cave a couple months ago, we found the skull of a woman in there, a woman who died–who may have been murdered– about the same time as the explosion. You wouldn't happen to have an idea who the woman was and what she was doing in there?"

"That was long before I was born, Detective."

"Could it be some heretic or some woman of the night your grandfather wanted to get rid of?"

Chapter 20

A STRANGER wriggled his way out of a Prius that he had parked at the side of the Jamestown Kwik Trip. He shook out the knots from having driven too long. As he did, he saw Wads over by one of the gas islands throwing out handfuls of oil dry and ambled over. "Oil spill?" he asked.

"Someone was in here on a Harley. Those damn things leak oil whenever and wherever they stop."

"Harley drivers say their bikes are just marking their territory."

Wads glanced up at the stranger smirking, the stranger in wrinkled slacks and a short-sleeved knit shirt. "Are you some smart-mouthed hog lover?"

"You having a bad night?"

"Cleaning up oil leaks on my concrete, yeah."

The stranger, grinning even more, stuck out his hand. "I'm your new district manager."

"Ohmigod, I'm sorry." Wads brushed his fingers on his jeans before he clamped onto the stranger's hand. "John Wadkowski. What happened to Charlene?"

"Last week, she went with another convenience-store chain that shall not be named."

"And you?"

"Leon Decker. Call me LD."

Wads tossed a look at the oil dry that had caked up as it absorbed the puddle by pump eight. "Let me sweep this up, then I'll give you the tour."

He took a shovel and broom to the mess, whisking the oily crumbles into the shovel and dumping them into a waste barrel on wheels. After Wads had the mess up, he spritzed the area with degreaser, to remove the stain, then mopped that up with paper toweling.

Decker shoved his hands in his back pockets as he watched. "I've never seen anybody go to this much trouble. Oil dry, yes, but degreaser, never."

"On the night shift, LD, this store's mine, inside and out. We keep it clean." Wads pitched the toweling into the barrel and followed that with the shovel and broom. The tub of oil dry he hung on a hook inside the barrel and trundled off to a storage building behind the store.

When he got back, he found Decker not by the pumps but inside, filling a cup at the coffee station and talking to Chow, Chow whose hair stood up in a well-moussed Mohawk colored alternately green and yellow. "See you've met my right hand," Wads said.

"She speaks well of you." Decker sampled the brew. "Good stuff. Make it fresh every half hour?"

"That's what the manual of standards calls for."

Chow excused herself and broke away to checkout a customer waiting at the front counter with a beverage and a sack of cinnamon rolls.

Wads spread his hands. "Want the tour?"

Decker shook his head. "I'm a quick study. I've seen everything I need. Can we go to your office?"

"Sure." Wads led the way to the back of the store. There he swept a short stack of cleaning supplies catalogs off the spare chair and gestured for Decker to take it.

After the district manager got himself comfortable, Wads went on to his own chair, straightening some paperwork on his deck as he sat down. "You been with the company long?"

"Six years, in Iowa." Decker cradled his cup in his hands, as if he were warming them. His gaze went to a trophy, a miniature wheelchair mounted on a cheap plastic pedestal. "What's this?"

Wads pulled the trophy to himself. "It's a long story."

"I got time."

"Back in the spring, I wrecked my ankle, and I was supposed to be in a Dancing With The Stars thing fundraiser for the library. Well, I wanted to beg off."

"Ah-ha, and your partner didn't let you."

Wads laughed, shaking his head as he did. "No, she made me do our routine in the show, all right, me in a wheelchair, and darned if we didn't win third place."

"I would have liked to have seen that."

Wads slid the trophy back to where it had resided. "You can if you want. It's on You Tube."

Decker caressed his chin. "Well, back to business. John, how many of our stores have you been to?"

"A couple. And call me Wads."

"All right. See any differences between those and yours?"

"Not much, as I recall."

Decker came forward. He propped an elbow on his knee. "Wads, you've got a good store here. You do a good business. I know, I've studied the spreadsheets. But this store is old, as old as Old MacDonald, the oldest in my district. I don't know why Charlene didn't push to remodel it, update it, but I sure am. Whaddaya think?"

"What would we get?"

"I'll recommend a whole new front end—a new beverage area, a better display for our bakery and meat products, and our top-of-the-line coffee station. We've got to replace that dinky one you've got. With the new station, you can have eight different kinds of hot coffee ready, plus you'll have a flavor shot machine and an espresso maker."

"That's the Café Karuba, right?"

Decker threw him an okay sign.

"I've seen that on the company's website."

"Wads, you'll knock the pins out from under Mickey D, Dunkin Donuts, and every other store here that's pushing coffee."

Wads tilted his head to the side. "I don't know. Our Swedes, they want only one kind and that's strong and black."

On one of the screens above and behind Decker, two teens in dusters and Rich Homie Quan ball caps bailed out of a low-rider pickup. They wandered toward the store and inside where they split, one going to the coffee station, the other making his way to the back. On another screen, Wads saw that teen wave to Chow, apparently asking her to come help him find something.

On a third screen, Chow left the checkout counter and glanced at the teen turning from the coffee station to the meat cooler, that teen reaching inside for a package of cheese brats.

Chow went on.

Wads jacked his pointer finger at Decker, then up to the bank of screens. "You ever see anything on the closed-circuit monitors in one of our stores and say to yourself something's about to go to hell here?"

Decker craned around. As he did, Chow on a near screen threw a teen on the floor. She gave a chop to his arm and left him screaming as she raced away to the front. There she kicked out into a spikes-up baseball slide and clipped the legs out from under the second teen running for the door. He fell and she came up and just as fast came down on the teen's back with her knee.

"Boss, get out here!"

Wads shoved his desk phone at Decker. "Call nine-one-one."

He slammed through the door, grabbed the near teen by the collar, the teen squalling, clutching his arm, and dragged him up the aisle to where Chow held the other pinned to the floor.

She latched onto a flailing hand and twisted it up behind her teen's back. "It's the old distraction trick. One guy distracts the clerk so the other can steal everything in sight. Boss, in this kid's pockets inside his coat? Not Ding Dongs, but steaks. Our steaks."

Chapter 21

WADS AND DECKER pushed Chow ahead of them into The Library, Wads calling out to Barb Larson, "A giant diet Sprite for Cat and put a cherry in it. Better, two scoops of skinny ice cream. Make it a Sprite float."

Larson shot a fist full of fingers in the air. "What's the occasion?"

"You should have seen her tonight. A couple shoplifters came in, and Cat mopped the floor with them."

The trio settled like grackles on stools at the bar.

Larson, as she filled a mug, gave a jerk of her head toward Decker. "Who's the new guy?"

Wads reached over the bar for a cleaning rag and went at wiping up a ring of beer left by some previous customer's overly full stein. "My new district manager, LD Decker."

Larson tucked a straw in the float before she set it and a spoon in front of Chow. She then elbowed Decker's elbow as he leaned on the bar, his hands folded together. "What'll it be, new district manager?"

"How about a black cow? I still have to drive home."

"Wherezat?"

"Madison. Just moved there."
"From where?"
"Mason City."
"Iowa?"
"Right."
"River City in *The Music Man*."
"You got it."
"Back in high school, I played Ethel Toffelmier of the Pickalittle Ladies." Larson went into the Pickalittle number, singing a half-dozen bars, ending with a modest laugh. "Those were good times. Well, one black cow it is and for your host one Muscle Milk, strawberry-flavored."
Wads winked at Larson. "Tonight make it Cookies an' Cream."
"Oh, living high, are we?" She turned to the back bar where she snapped the cap off a Gray's Root Beer. Larson poured another mug half full before she dug into the ice cream bucket. As she worked, she glanced up at the mirror, at the image of Zigman coming through the front door toting his ever-present leather case.
Zigman slipped it up on the bar and parked himself on the stool next to Wads. He gave a wave to Chow in the mirror. "Cat, you are the talk of the police station and the sheriff's department. Black belt, right, in what?"
"Wushu." She sipped at her float. "My father, he made me take classes in Shaolin wushu. Said I needed to know how to protect myself."
"Paid off."
"I guess."

Zigman leaned into Wads. "Remind me never, never ever again to give her a hard time."

"I can do that. What's got you up so late?"

"Oh, a burglary out in the county."

"You wouldn't stop in here to tell us about that."

"No." Zigman unzipped his case. "You wanted to know about the disposition of the manslaughter case against Gilcrest for killing your great uncle, remember? I found the record." He laid his case open so Wads could read a yellowed document. "Gilcrest didn't show on the day of the trial. Skipped town. Disappeared apparently. There's no record of him in the county after that date. However–"

Wads looked up from the paltry notes of the court clerk. "However what?"

"–Chrisco had a crew in leveling land on his farm for a parking lot for that speakeasy of his. They uncovered a grave."

"And?"

"Found a skeleton of a man, complete, all the bones there." Zigman made a pistol of his index finger and thumb. He cocked his thumb and fired. "Bullet hole in the skull."

Wads tapped out a tattoo on the bar. "You're thinking this is Gilcrest and that my grandfather–"

"Wads, I'm not thinking anything. But I am wondering–"

"What?"

"–if there's a connection between the woman shot in the cave and Gilcrest being shot outside the cave."

Chapter 22

WADS AND ZIGMAN tilted back in their chairs, their feet up on the desk in Wads's Kwik Trip office, he sipping from a bottle of Joe, Zigman tipping up a stubby Cherry Coke. When nothing more came out, Zigman put the mouth of the bottle to his eye and peered inside.

Wads held up his bottle of water. "You sure sucked that down in a hurry."

"Well, you hogged the conversation, so what else could I do?"

A voice interrupted, trickling out of the computer on the desk, announcing 'You've got mail.'

Zigman glanced at the machine, puzzlement tickling an eyebrow. "You're still getting email from Nineteen Ninety-five?"

"If it ain't broke—" Wads tapped an icon on the screen and an envelope opened. From it, up floated a card, all accompanied by an oomph band playing "Roll Out the Barrel."

Wads swung his feet down and hunched forward, the better to see the message. "Listen to this: 'Ye olde friend of the Bullets Chrisco Speakeasy, ye are hereby invited to come hither and lay thine eye upon the arrival of ye speakeasy's most magnificent interior by caravan on the morrow, nine in the a.m. most prompt. C.C., one Howard Zigman."

Zigman flicked his empty away at a recycle can in the corner. The plastic bottle hit the rim, bounced up, and fell, not in the can, but on the floor where Zigman scuttled after it. "I thought this was a stick-build job."

"Apparently not. You want me to pick you up?"

"Eight-thirty? Will ye, olde friend, have thine eyes open?"

"I'll clothespin my lids to my eyebrows."

THE CLOCK on the screen in the dash of Wads's dually read eight fifty-five and forty seconds when he and Zigman turned off the county road and onto the gravel drive that led to Monte Chrisco's farmstead. They tooled up to the house where their host sat on a side porch, sucking down a cup of coffee, a wolfhound at his side, looking as if he were about to charge out and devour any stranger who dared step on the grass.

After Wads cut his pickup's engine, he leaned out the window. "I didn't see any Beware The Dog sign. When did you get the beast?"

"Brought him up from Chi-town yesterday." Chrisco touched the dog's shoulders and pointed down. The wolfhound responded by flopping on his belly. He then laid his chin on his crossed paws, his eyes casting a most sorrowful gaze at nothing.

"Safe to get out?"

"It is now."

Wads and Zigman dismounted. As they went on toward the house, gabbing, the rumbling sound of heavy diesels–semis trucking up the county road–drifted their way, the lead semi's engine blatting as it rapped down, the truck slowing. Then came a blistering series of bangs, like gunfire.

Wads and Zigman jerked around, and Chrisco leaped from his porch, his dog with him. The four raced toward the road where the lead semi ground to a halt at the driveway entrance, all eighteen tires flat.

Two men clambered down from the big rig. The driver, built like a wrestler and chewing a cud, huffed around the front while his relief trotted back along the side of the trailer, scanning the pavement. He stooped, picked up something, and underhanded it to his partner hustling over to Chrisco and company.

The driver snatched the object from the air and held it out. "Wouldn'tcha know, a gawddamn jack. I quit hauling fer the coal companies in West Virginny to get away from these."

He tossed the jack to Chrisco.

Chrisco examined it–two six-penny nails bent ninety degrees and welded together at the bend point–before he passed it to Zigman who showed it to Wads.

Wads rolled the object in his hand. "Kinda like a kid's jack, isn't it, only this thing'll punch a hole in any tire that rolls over it. We didn't hit any."

The driver pitched up an eyebrow. "Who you?"

"John Wadkowski. I got here a bit ahead of you." He handed the object back to Zigman. "My pard here's a detective with the sheriff's department."

The driver spit a cheekful of tobacco juice to the side. "Detective, looks like you got yerself a crime to solve. Somebody doesn't want us to deliver our loads here."

Zigman jiggled the jack in his hand. "But you are here."

"Uh-huh, and at a cost of eighteen new tires. You know how much that is? And then there's the lost time for my drivers who can't get around me to unload. We're union, so that ain't cheap."

Chrisco pulled Wads off to the side. He took out his cell. "I need help here, buddy boy. Who do I call?"

"Pomps."

"Who'd you say?"

"Pomps. They do road service for big rigs. They'll have everything you need–tires, rims, the works."

"The number?"

"Count, I'm not the telephone information girl. Google it."

A DEPUTY with a metal detector walked the shoulder of the road, searching for jacks not easily seen, while four men from the road service company worked with the speed of an Indianapolis pit crew, changing out the busted tires for new on the lead semi.

The driver, Dingo Mays, watched them. "Fast, ain't they," he said to Zigman. "As I was sayin', somebody or several somebodies musta pitched that sack o' jacks out on the pavement just before we come along. My bet is they had a helper down around the bend there—" He sighted in the direction from which the caravan had come. "—watchin' for us. He seen us an' called his buddies an' they salted the road."

Zigman jotted a note on the back of a log sheet he'd bummed from Mays. "We didn't see anybody or any vehicles when we came by."

"Hell, Detective, I wouldn't be standin' at the side of the road with a bag o' jacks in my hand, either. I'd be out there in the cornfield a couple rows deep where you couldn't see me."

A crime scene tech pushed his way out of the cornfield and into the ditch. He came on up, swinging an iPad, to Zigman. "Detective, I've got something for you."

He flipped the cover over so Zigman could see the screen, the image on it a boot print with a ruler beside it. The tech swept his hand over the screen. "What we've got here is Big Foot, a size sixteen hoof."

"Manny, you're kidding me."

"Nope. There's another set of boot prints the same size out there. The perps knew they were going to leave footprints, so they decided not to leave anything we could use to identify them. Thus the humongous galoshes they wore. However—"

Zigman brightened. "You've got something?"

The tech held up three fingers, then folded two into his palm. "One, by the length of the stride, I can tell you one perp is about six feet tall, give or take an inch or two."

"The second thing?"

"Your second perp is a shrimp, someone around four-ten."

"You're on a roll, Manny. Keep going."

The tech brought a baggie out of his jacket pocket, a baggie half full with wet dirt. He shook the baggie. "One of your bad guys had to relieve himself or herself. Real strong whiff of urine out there, so we can get us some DNA."

Zigman slapped the tech's shoulder. "You, my man, are the best."

"I'd appreciate it if you'd tell my boss, and tell her I could use a raise."

The head of the Pomps crew came over, wiping his hands on a cleaning rag. "Dingo, you're good to go just as soon as I run your credit card through my Square."

Mays hauled a massive leather wallet out of his back pocket, the wallet chained to his belt. He picked around inside until he found a company credit card. This he passed to the Pomps man who swiped it through the reader on his smart phone.

"Now if you'd just sign the screen with your trigger finger—" The Pomps man handed the cell to Mays who John Henry'd the screen and handed the cell back.

The Pomps man waggled his phone. "Want a printout?"

"'Preciate it."

"I'll make you one at my truck and bring it back to you." He trotted away.

After he disappeared, Mays spun his hand above his head, a start-'em-up signal to his relief in the cab, then flagged him into the driveway. Other semis snorted to life and followed, four in all, all flatbeds carrying crates stacked ten feet high. One exception, tail-end Charlie, a lowboy transporting forklifts, a car shrouded in canvas, and a tow tractor with Southwest Airlines stenciled on the side.

Mays hopped aboard the lowboy as it bumbled by.

CHRISCO, at a parking lot a hundred yards short of the cave, guided the semis into a half-circle.

Engines shut down and crews descended, again except for tail-end Charlie. He dropped his trailer and drove away, off to the side.

Crews massed like ants, several men driving the forklifts and the tow tractor off the lowboy, the forklifts operators going after crates on the first flatbed and shuttling them back to the lowboy where they restacked them no more than five feet high, measured from the ground.

The driver of the tow tractor hooked the lowboy to his rig and waited for the trans-loading to be completed.

Chrisco stood admiring all the busy-ness. To Wads beside him, he said, "Remember those plans I showed you? Even before I met with your county zoning staff, I had shops in Chicago building the speakeasy in sections that they could crate and ship up. In the cave, I've got crews of carpenters, electricians, and plumbers waiting for my man on the tow tractor to haul the lowboy in."

Wads rubbed at the side of his face. "The entrance to the cave, is it wide enough?"

"I measured it again this morning. Eight feet ten inches, an inch to spare on either side of the trailer. The crew'll uncrate the sections—they're all numbered—move the sections where they need to be and snap them together like Legos, even the dance floor and the mirror over the bar."

Wads watched the tow-tractor driver start the lowboy creeping toward the cave. "I've got to know, Zigman asked me why you didn't build it here."

"It would have taken too long. Had I done that, I wouldn't be able to open until next spring. But by working with the builders and the craftsmen in Chicago, I can open next week."

"Count, weren't you taking one honkin'-big gamble? The zoning board could have turned you down."

"Wasn't gonna happen."

"Come on, you couldn't know that."

Chrisco squared around to Wads. "Buddy boy, I'm from Illinois. I bought the planning staff so they'd recommend the zoning change."

"You bribed them?"

"I made an investment." Chrisco gave an FDR jut to his jaw. "If the board had voted the change down, I would have then bought them, so I'd get a yes vote on the second go-round."

Chapter 23

WADS SAT in his favorite booth in The Library, paging through a book he'd taken down from the shelves, "Bottoms Up: A Toast to Wisconsin's Historic Bars and Breweries." He stopped on a photo spread about Dawn's Never Inn, a bar on the second floor of an old hotel in Hurley.

Barb Larson leaned over his shoulder. She brushed his ear with her cheek. "What have you found there, big boy?"

"Look at this. They've got a moose made from old beer cans in this place. Maybe if you did something special, you could get The Library in the next edition."

"Like what?"

"Like make a life-size dairy cow out of beer cans."

"Or empty Muscle Milk bottles." She puffed a warm breath into Wads's ear.

He scrunched up, so she played with his earlobe. "You could come to my place after closing time, and I could really get you going."

Zigman wandered in from the cool of the night. When he spotted Wads and Larson, Larson draped around Wads's shoulders, he sauntered up and slid onto the opposite booth seat. "Am I witnessing the beginning of something lascivious here?"

Wads clamped onto Zigman's arm. "Thank you, thank you, thank you. You saved me."

Larson ran her fingers through Wads's hair. "Zig, isn't he cute when he blushes?"

"Oh my, yes, cute. I hate to interrupt."

Wads squeezed Zigman's arm. "It's all right. Please interrupt. Pleeese."

"If you'll buy me a Coke."

Wads looked up at Larson. "A Cherry Coke for my savior. How about it?"

She departed for the bar.

Zigman waited until Larson was well away before he unzipped his leather case and laid it open on the table. "I had a deputy drive my baggie of dirt and pee up to the state crime lab with a rush order. For once, they processed it right away." He turned the case to Wads. "It's male."

"Match anything in the state data base?"

"Afraid not. However, now if we can net us a suspect, we can run his DNA against this. Get a match and—" Zigman thumbed over his shoulder, like a baseball umpire calling a player out.

The front door swung open once more. This time Chrisco stepped in. He flagged Larson coming away from the bar. "Sweets, how about you put a Scud Missile on that order for me? Bacardi One Fifty-one and cinnamon schnapps."

"You got it." With that, Larson turned back.

Chrisco went on to Wads's booth. "Got room for one more?"

Zigman slid further in.

Wads gazed at the new arrival as he sat down. "You just coming off the job?"

"Hoo-yah. We got it all inside and most of it assembled."

"When are the building inspectors coming?"

Chrisco waggled his trigger finger. "They've been with us all day and night–building, electrical, plumbing. I paid extra for the immediate service."

"You bribed them?"

"No, I paid the county for their wages so my job would go to the top of the list. I'm not a crook, Wads."

"So how'd you come out?"

"So far, not problem one. Where I come from, inspectors would have found twenty violations that didn't exist so you'd pony up with an envelope of cash."

Chrisco stopped, his hand cupped and on the table. Larson set his drink in his hand and placed the Cherry Coke in front of Zigman.

Wads flipped to another section in "Bottoms Up." He turned it to Chrisco. "You're building a gangsters' bar, I'm just curious, how come you didn't model it after The Little Bohemia up in Manitowish?"

Chrisco danced his fingers over the pictures. "I considered it. The FBI shootout with John Dillinger and his gang there in 'Twenty-seven, that appealed to me. But The Bohemia is so North Woods, it's just not what I wanted. You saw the way our back bar fits into the stone wall of the cave. That's special. And the stone of the canopy and the way we rigged the lights to show it all off, no one can match that."

"Count, if you'd done The Little Bohemia, you could have invited Johnny Depp to the grand opening, to come in the suit and fedora he wore in 'Public Enemies'."

Chrisco tossed back a part of his drink. "Who's to say he won't be with us?"

Larson's jaw dropped. "You invited him?"

Chrisco winked.

Larson squeezed in next to Wads. "Hon, he's invited Johnny Depp—Jack Sparrow? John Dillinger?"

"Tonto? Oh, no, that movie was awful. Idiot hairstyle for Depp, and they made him up like a ghost. But now in 'Public Enemies'—"

Chrisco slipped an envelope to Larson and one to Zigman. "Your invitations to the grand opening. You each can bring a guest, and for you, sweets, I know that's Wads."

Wads closed his book. "When you doing this?"

"Saturday eve next week. You'll be with the movers and shakers, the pacesetters and decision makers, the county and city's elite one hundred. By the way, it's black tie."

Chapter 24

SOMEONE AT THE SIDE of the road flashed up in the headlights of Larson's car, a man clearly now holding a placard that read 'Booze'. Then beyond him another person with another placard, this one reading 'Ahead', followed by three more people and three more placards—'Pass', 'On', 'By'.

Larson glanced at Wads in the buddy seat. "What is this?"

"Twenty-first century version of the Burma Shave signs. Somebody doesn't want anybody stopping at the Count's speakeasy."

Larson slowed for the turnoff. As she did, her headlights picked up two policemen holding back a cluster of picketers waving their own signs—'Alcohol an abomination', 'Love God and coffee, not whiskey and gin', and 'Enter here for your ticket to Hell.'

Larson rolled onto a graveled lane. "I cannot believe this."

"I know who to talk to if you'd like them to picket The Library."

She swatted Wads, and he howled, feigning injury.

"You are a ham." Larson guided her car on past Monte Chrisco's house and farm buildings, past a hayfield, and over a rise that opened onto a massive, lighted parking lot.

A man in a yellow safety vest flagged her forward and pointed toward another person in a safety vest down a line of parked cars who waved her into an open space.

Larson cut the motor and dropped the ignition key into her clutch purse. She rubbed Wads's knee, cooing to him, "You're not upset, are you, that I drove? After all, I had the invitation."

He wanted to put his hand over hers, but held back. "Have I complained?"

"No, but I know you wanted to, particularly when that spring punched up through the seat."

He rubbed his hip where he'd been speared. "Barb, you need a better car than this old beater."

"Hey, it's all I can afford on my bartender's salary. Now if I win the Lotto—"

"And the chances of that are what?" Wads forced a grin as he clambered out of Larson's Suzuki, what to him was little more than an oversized toy. He unbent himself to come upright and brushed the wrinkles out of his tux while Larson slipped out of her side of the two-seater.

She came around to him, she in a short-skirted, sleeveless black dress with elbow-length gloves and fishnet hosiery, the dress shimmering with rhinestones. Larson tucked her arm in Wads's, and the two hoofed it off to a top-down, low-rider Packard waiting to shuttle them to the entrance of the cave and on inside.

The driver, in chauffeur's togs, opened the door to the backseat for them. "You do remember the password?"

Larson waved the invitation.

"Very good."

"So everything's ready for the big night, huh?" Wads asked after the driver got in and started the car rolling.

The driver glanced up in his mirror. "At least out here. Inside, we've got our fingers crossed."

"Have you taxied in any famous people yet?"

"The mayor and his wife about ten minutes ago. Another driver got our state's lieutenant governor–Missus Kleefisch–and her bodyguard, big bruiser of a state trooper."

He stopped at a clapboard shack that stood beside the gated entrance to the cave. A portal slid open and someone asked, "Password?"

The driver gave a nod at Larson.

She leaned toward the portal and read from the invitation, "Leinenkugel Oktoberfest."

"Spell that."

"Leinenkugel?"

"Oktoberfest."

"O-k-t-o–"

"Enter. Honey, a 'c' would have kept you out."

The gates swung inward and out of the way, and the driver eased the car forward. He called out to his passengers, "Low ceiling. Watch you heads."

Wads and Larson ducked. After the car cleared the low entrance and rolled inside to where the roof of the cave rose, they straightened up. Ahead and to the side loomed up a gleaming yellow convertible, the antique bathed in lights.

Larson oooed. "Can we get out and see it?"

The driver again glanced up in his mirror. "Sure, lady. But if I let you out here, you'll have to hike the rest of the way. See, I gotta get back out to the parking lot for my next load."

"That's okay."

He stopped the Packard.

Wads got out and held the door for Larson. After she stepped down, the driver sped away, if seven miles an hour can be called speeding.

Wads and Larson strolled over to the edge of the lights. Inside, next to a camera, stood someone in a tux, someone with multi-colored spiked hair.

"Cat?" Wads asked.

The person swivelled around, grinning. "How about this, boss, I've got a weekend gig. I'm the photographer at this station."

"Mighty fine station. What kind of a car is this?"

Chow swept her hand back, as a model would at an auto show. "A Nineteen Twenty-two Kissel Goldbug. The information card they gave me says that Amelia Earhart owned a car like this. You probably knew her."

"Cat, I'm old, but I'm not that old."

Larson clutched Wads's arm. "Can we have our picture taken in the car?"

"I'm game."

Chow opened the driver's door, but before she let anyone in, she stepped toward the rear wheel. "I want to show you something." She opened a compartment in the side of the car, behind the seat, and a second seat slid out. "This is called an outrigger seat or a mother-in-law seat. Some, I was told, even called it a suicide seat. There's one just like it on the other side of the car, so four people could ride. Isn't that something?"

Larson pushed Wads toward the driver's seat. For herself, she perched up on the outrigger seat, winking at Wads as she settled. "Shows my legs off better, don't you think?"

He looked back, and his eyebrows rose.

Chow returned to her camera. She peered at the screen and then at Wads. "Boss, would you put your elbow over the door? That's it. Now lean out a bit and one hand on the steering wheel."

Larson crossed her legs at the ankles and turned a tad, to give the camera a better view of her bust.

A golf cart whooshed up with Chrisco at the wheel. He hopped out and put his hands on Larson's shoulders. "Should we make this a three-shot?"

She looked up at him. "Sure."

Wads called back his agreement.

Chrisco leaned to the side. He put his face cheek-to-cheek with Larson's.

Smiles, flash.

And two more, after which Chow raised her hand. "That's it. You can pick up prints at the bar in five minutes and a thumb drive, so you can upload your picture to Facebook and Instagram."

Chrisco squeezed Larson's shoulders, then stepped around to open the door for Wads. "Isn't this car something? Cat may have told you that Amelia

Earhart had a Gold Bug just like this one, same year. It's in a museum out in Denver. Try as I might, they wouldn't loan it to me."

Wads gazed over the cockpit and forward along the top line of the hood, as if he were taking the car in for the first time. "So where'd you get this one?"

"How about this? Just up the road, from the Wisconsin Automotive Museum."

"Classic." Wads wedged himself out of the Gold Bug that, for interior space, was not much larger than Larson's car, but for length appeared to be a boat.

Chrisco caressed the winged hood ornament. "This was thee hot sports car of its day. But let me show you what else I brought in. Come on, hop in my golf cart."

He gave Larson the passenger seat. That stuck Wads with the rear-facing back seat.

Chrisco stepped down on the electric's accelerator. That slipped the cart away with little more than a whir. "To establish a perspective here," he said, waving his hand as he drove, "Gold Bugs like that one sell for about a hundred forty thousand dollars when they come up for auction. Now the car we're coming up on, a Duesenberg Boattail Speedster built in Nineteen Thirty-three, that one sold last for just under a half-mill."

He slowed the golf cart to a walk as he came up on the Boattail and a cluster of people ogling it.

Wads twisted to the side for a better view. "Whose is it?"

"Anonymous. But I know Mister Anonymous, so he let me ship it in. Now this next car–I told you I'd get Al Capone's car here and I did—it's Capone's Nineteen Twenty-eight Cadillac Town Sedan. He had it tricked out like the squad cars the Chicago Police used—green and black color scheme, flashing lights, siren. He even had a police radio receiver put in it, the first ever to be in a civilian car. Whatever Al wanted, Al got."

Chrisco stopped the golf cart. He tweaked the horn and motioned to the people who looked his way to move aside. "This Caddy's one a helluva car," he said to Larson, "three thousand pounds of armor plating, window glass an inch thick so it's bulletproof. Crank the windows up a little more and there are holes in the glass so you can stick the barrel of your machine gun out and blast away at whoever's shooting at you. And that's not all. If you're being chased, you can drop the back window and spray the chase car with your machine gun." Chrisco turned to Wads. "Buddy boy, you and your moll, we can take a picture of the two of you standing beside Al's car. I stress 'standing beside the car.' The owner won't let me let anyone sit inside."

Wads rotated his shoulder, to loosen it. "You wouldn't happen to know the price tag on it? Just curious."

"A bit more than a third of a mill. That's what the current owner paid for it two years ago."

"Another Mister Anonymous, I suppose."

"Right. Anyone who's got a car like this in his private collection doesn't want it noised around. Would you like a picture? We can give you a couple props."

"Sure, why not?" Wads stepped down. He took Larson by her gloved hand and guided her over to the Capone Cadillac where the photographer's assistant handed Wads a Panama hat and Larson a Tommy gun, then positioned them next to the car.

Three quick flashes, followed by instructions on picking up the picture and thumb drive, and Chrisco, Wads, and Larson toured away to the next stop, a side cave rigged to look like a parking garage in Chicago on Valentine's Day, Nineteen Twenty-nine. Nine men hugged the wall while four others held them at gunpoint, two dressed as Chicago policemen.

Chrisco stopped at the crime scene tape that cordoned off the faux garage from the speakeasy and waved over a young woman in a tailored suit and fedora. He gestured to the tableau. "Everything ready?"

"Absolutely, Mister Chrisco." The woman saw Wads and fluttered her fingers at him. "Remember me?"

Wads pointed his index finger at her. "Yes, the now-married polka dancer, Anna Doskocil. No, no, it's Deleatorre now, isn't it?"

"Right, I'm Mister Chrisco's director of media and entertainment, my first real job in three years."

"Good for you."

"Thanks."

Chrisco, like the man was—in charge—guided the golf cart away along a track that kept him and his passengers close to the wall as they buzzed around the table area of the speakeasy and the dance floor. There clusters of people gyrated to the beat and music of an Earth, Wind, and Fire tribute band playing and singing "September."

In the area where the drivers of the shuttle cars turned around for their trips back to the parking lot, Chrisco whisked his golf cart into a slot posted with a sign that identified it as 'For Da Great White Shark'.

He hopped out and hustled Wads and Larson to the bar. "What can we get for you?"

Wads pitched up his volume to make himself heard of the "ba-dee-ya" lyrics. "Cranberry Sierra Mist for Barb and a water for me."

Chrisco snagged a bartender. He twiddled his fingers at his guests. "One cranberry Sierra Mist and one water for my friends, and a Honey Pepper Whiskey for me."

"Right away, Mister Chrisco."

Wads scratched at his ear. "Did I hear that right, honey pepper whiskey?"

"Yeah, that's Tennessee whiskey, Kentucky bourbon, and clover honey with a hit of chili pepper that leaves a tingly bite on the tongue. You can't get it in Wisconsin, so I had two cases flown in from the bottler, and guess where he is, Newton, Pennsylvania. The next flavored whiskey they're coming out with is maple bacon."

Wads cringed.

Larson touched Chrisco's arm. "I should tell you, my boss—he owns The Library—he's none too happy with you opening up here. You're competition, see. So he says he may have to have you rubbed out."

"Really?"

"I think he's joking. Still and all—"

The bartender set the drinks in front of the trio and hurried away to other customers. Chrisco ignored his honey pepper whiskey. Instead, he gazed off at a Packard low-rider making its way to the turn-around. At the turn-around, it stopped and let off two passengers, a gangster and his moll or so they looked, he in a black overcoat, fedora, and leather gloves and toting a Thompson machine gun, she in a knockout sleeveless red dress, the neckline plunging to the navel.

Chrisco hustled to them.

Larson pulled Wads in close so he could hear her over the pulsing beat of the band. "That girl back at the Cadillac—"

"Yeah?"

"—did you see that?"

"See what?"

"She's got a gun under her arm. I saw the bulge in her coat."

"Maybe it's just a part of the gangster-getup theme for the place."

"Yeah, maybe that's it."

Chrisco came back, escorting his latest guests.

Larson, bug-eyed, dropped her Mist. She lunged at the man, hugged him, and planted a massive kiss on his cheek. She screamed, "Johnny Depp!"

Depp wiped at the smear of lipstick. "A reception like this, I've gotta come to Wisconsin more often."

Larson twisted to Wads while still clinging to Depp's arm. "My God, it's Johnny Depp. I can't believe it. Wads, take a picture of us, please? Pleeese?"

Wads grubbed his cell from his pocket. While he framed the shot, Depp struck a movie pose, the stock of his machine gun braced against one hip, his free arm around Larson's waist. She obliged and moved her hands high on his shoulder, clasping them together. They both faced the camera phone, she with a smile fit for a toothpaste commercial, he with a Jack Sparrow arch to his eyebrow.

Wads tapped the TAKE button, and his cell clicked.

Chrisco stepped in. "I hate to break this up, but it's showtime. Let's all go up on the stage. Johnny, I'll introduce you."

The five moved away from the bar with Chrisco cleaving a path through the crowd.

When finally on stage, Wads saw Zigman and his wife off to the side, Zigman with a look of 'what am I doing here' on his face. Wads hooked up with him. "Wondered where you were."

"Marty and I got here a bit early. The Count said he wanted us up here for the opening ceremonies. I don't know why."

Chrisco, towing Depp and his date, moved out in front of the band to a microphone. There he waved to the audience for silence. When the conversations trailed off, he pulled the microphone in close. "Welcome, everybody, to Bullets Chrisco's Speakeasy."

Modest applause came from the crowd.

"Thank you for coming, and a particular thank you to Johnny Depp. Johnny Depp—John Dillinger!"

Chrisco threw his hand out toward Depp, and an explosion of applause greeted the actor.

Depp stepped forward. He swung his machine gun over his head as the applause continued.

A blistering blaze of gunfire ripped off from the side, from the Clark Street garage set, the tableau alive, Capone's four gunmen mowing down Bugs Moran's gang. Some in the audience screamed and others ducked to get out of the way whatever was happening.

From the corner of his eye, Wads caught Anna Deleatorre slipping away from the fake massacre, a pistol in her hand, leveled, aimed at Chrisco. He threw himself at Depp and the Count, creamed them both as one last shot rang out, igniting a new round of commotion.

Zigman stepped forward, his own gun drawn. He shouted to Wads scrambling to his knees, "Where's the shooter?"

Wads motioned to Deleatorre running for the other side cave that housed the kitchen and storage areas.

Zigman whipped a Thirty-eight from his ankle holster and tossed it to Wads, and they both burst away from the stage. They slammed through the kitchen door into chaos—cooks aghast, waiters huddled under prep tables, a backdoor open to a storeroom.

Zigman and Wads leaped over dropped trays of steaks and baked potatoes, slipped in spilled tomato bisque, and skidded to a stop at the door.

Zigman crouched. He edged through, into the storeroom, scanning ahead. "Shooter! I'm a sheriff's detective. The only way you're gonna get out of this alive is to throw your gun out where I can see it and come out with your fingers locked behind your head."

Silence.

Wads inched in beside Zigman.

Zigman glanced at him. "Whaddayah think?"

"I hate games of hide-and-seek."

"He's not giving us much choice."

"He's a she."

"Pardon?"

"Anna Deleatorre. I saw her. Remember her from The Library, the Czech girl? At the bachelorette party? Anna Doskocil?"

Zigman stared at Wads. "Doskocil? What the hell's going on?"

"All I know is what I saw. She had a gun out and aimed at Chrisco."

"All right, let us go seek. Do your best Danny Reagan and check the aisles on your side. I'll get those on mine. She's gotta be here somewhere."

Both crept forward.

Wads popped his head and gun around into the first aisle as Zigman did the same on his side of the storeroom.

Nothing.

Second aisle.

Nothing.

Third aisle.

More of nothing.

Wads sat back on his heels. "I really, really hate this," he mouthed to Zigman. "Last aisle."

He motioned for Zigman to peek around his side. When Zigman moved, Wads poked his head and gun around into his aisle. "Not here. She can't have evaporated."

"I've a door at the end of my aisle. She must have gone out that way." Zigman tapped his chest and gestured from himself to the door.

He moved away, but Wads latched onto the hem of his tux jacket, gave a yank on it.

Zigman glanced back, and Wads jacked his finger at a pair of light switches to the side of the door. "Let's see what we've got."

He eased up and read the tags: STOREROOM and CAVE FLOODS.

Wads peered down at Zigman on one knee, ready to open the door and spring through. "I'll kill the lights in here. You go out the door in the dark, and I'll hit the floodlights. If she's out there, the floods oughtta blind her."

"How far does this side cave go?"

"Don't know. Never been down there."

Zigman reached up for the door's lever handle. "All right, let's do it."

Wads snapped out the storeroom lights. In the darkness, the door opened and Wads sensed Zigman diving through the doorway and rolling. He snapped on the floods and, an instant later, popped his head and gun around the doorjamb.

Zigman came up, his gun leveled in both hands, steady, aimed forward, sweat beading up on his forehead. "Wads, there's nothing here. Just a pile of rocks at the end of the cave."

CHAPTER 25

SHERIFF'S DEPUTIES, around the speakeasy, busied themselves taking statements from grand opening guests and employees while, off to one side, a CSI tech poked through the trash of the Saint Valentine's massacre scene, searching for the shell from Anna Deleatorri's pistol. The shell had to be there, Zigman believed and Wads concurred, because Wads saw Deleatorre run before she had time to pick up the shell.

For themselves, Zigman and Wads stood at the end of the bar, hunched together with a third man, Zigman waggling his hand in front of the man's face. "Judge, what I need from you are an arrest warrant and a search warrant. We know who we're after."

Judge Harlan Fishbach, a fellow guest at the grand opening, doodled in a spill of water on the bar or perhaps it was gin. He dabbed his wet fingertip on his tongue. "Hm, vodka and not the best I've tasted."

"Are you going to be a critic of the booze here?"

"Well, at one time I was a connoisseur of fine liquors."

"Judge, you were, you know—"

"You can say it, the courthouse drunk. You were there the day the chief judge took me to the woodshed, and after that I got sober. But back to the business at hand, who are you after?"

"One Anna Doskocil Deleatorre."

"And you know her how?"

Zigman nudged Wads.

Wads, leaning on the bar, brought the fingers of his hands together in the form of a tent. "Judge, I've met the woman before and she's been at my store, and I saw her again earlier tonight here. So when she had a gun out and aimed at Chrisco, I knew who she was."

"You'll swear to that here and in court?"

"Absolutely."

Fishbach touched the back of Zigman's hand. "I'm satisfied, but I don't have any forms with me, obviously. We've got to do the paperwork right—"

"Or a smart defense lawyer'll get what we do thrown out."

"Exactly."

"Here I think I can help." Zigman scanned the crowd. When he spotted the CSI tech picking her way through the fake massacre, he stuck two fingers in his mouth and let out with a shriek of a whistle. The tech, startled, looked up, and Zigman waved her over.

She came, toting her soft shoulder bag. "Can I help you, Detective?"

"I need your iPad."

The tech brought out her tablet computer and handed it over.

Zigman fired it up. He clicked on the WiFi connection, then called up his office's forms file where he scrolled down to warrants. Zigman clicked on it. The form he wanted opened and he began typing.

Fishbach pulled in his bottle of Ginger ale while he studied Wads. "So Zig didn't see the shooter, this Deleatorre woman?"

"In all the ruckus, I guess he was looking in the wrong direction."

"What kind of weapon did she have?"

"A Glock maybe or something like it. Judge, I can't be sure. There was too much distance between us."

The tech brought a portable wireless printer out of her bag. She turned the machine on. Zigman touched the print icon on his screen, and the printer zipped out two copies.

"The arrest warrant," he said as he handed the pages to Fishbach. Zigman went back to tapping on the iPad's screen. He brought up a new file and scanned down it. "Wads, I couldn't find a land-line phone for Deleatorre, to get an address for the search warrant, but now I'm in a cellphone directory, and she's here. So is an Alexander Deleatorre with the same address. Is that her husband?"

"Uh-huh."

"Then we've got us a good address." Zigman called up the search warrant form and typed in the street address. Done, he tapped the print icon for two copies that he passed to Fishbach.

A second CSI tech squeezed in. He set his iPad up on the bar. "Got something for you."

"Yeah, Manny?"

"You didn't think there was a way out of that side cave where the kitchen is. My good man, there is, and I found it."

"And?"

"Thank your lucky stars, Detective, that I'm not a fat boy. I managed to wriggle through and outside." The tech touched his screen and up came two images, on one side a shoe print, on the other a tire impression. "The shoe, that's a size six woman's pump. The tire print, that's a Michelin Pilot Power Three. Sound familiar?"

"I'll say."

The tech wiped away the shoe print and brought up a second tire impression. "Remember this one? I found this out at the edge of the cornfield here a couple months ago. See the tear in both impressions?"

Zigman put on his half-moons. He leaned into the screen, tilting his head back as he did, to better to see the tear. "Wads, you said Deleatorre drives a Harley."

"Right, an Iron Eight Eighty-three."

"The Michelin is a Kawasaki tire, so we've got a problem here."

"Wait a minute." Wads put his hand on the tech's arm. "Did you find anything else?"

"Man, are you psychic?"

"Sometimes I think I am, but not really."

"I found a puddle of oil in the dirt where the bike had been parked. Scooped me up a sample for analysis."

Wads squeezed the tech's arm. "Manny, I know what you're going to find. That oil's from a leaky

Harley-Davidson. Zig, Anna's got Kawasaki tires on her bike."

"You think?"

"Hey, a little modification. It's something anybody could do. It's the only explanation that makes sense."

Zigman pulled the search warrants from Fishback's hands. "Judge, I'm going to run out a new warrant with the motorcycle on it and an assault rifle. That's the weapon that was used in the earlier shooting."

ZIGMAN AIMED his car's spotlight at a mailbox, illuminating a name in reflective letters, DELEATORRI, and a house number. He slowed and made the turnoff onto a paved drive that led through a cluster of oak trees, or so they appeared to be in the cool of the moon's light, to a McMansion. Zigman stopped under the columned portico, and he and Wads got out.

The two deputies who had followed them got out of their cruiser as well.

The four soldiered up to the door where Zigman punched the doorbell button. That set off a series of chimes that played the University of Wisconsin fight song. It also set off a dog, a little yapper by its burst of high-pitched barks.

"Hercules, quiet!"

A man's voice from inside.

A dead bolt slid and the door opened. There stood a man somewhat over six feet tall, in sweats and a t-shirt, clutching a Pomeranian in the crook of his arm, one hand clamped around the dog's muzzle. "If you're selling something, I'll let Hercules loose and he'll rip your leg off."

Zigman showed his badge.

The dog snarled at the movement, twisting and struggling in an effort to lunge at Zigman, but the man gripped the miniature terror that was more hair than dog even more tightly. "Sorry. He's possessive of his territory. Officer, what can I do for you?"

"This the Deleatorre residence?"

"Uh-huh."

"We'd like to talk with Anna Deleatorre. Is that your wife?"

"Right."

"She here?"

The Pomeranian erupted again, clawing this time at Deleatorre, dog and master in a wrestling match for dominance.

"Let me get rid of this beast," Deleatorre said through gritted teeth and backed away toward the interior of the house.

From behind Zigman, the deputies, and Wads came the rumbling sound of a Harley-Davidson moving up the driveway. They twisted around in time to see a black motorcycle speed up as it neared the sheriff's cruiser and the civilian Ford Fusion. The bike and its black-clad driver shot through the portico and away.

Zigman flung the search warrant at the closest deputy. "Make the search. I'm taking your cruiser."

He and Wads raced away to the Dodge Charger in police drag. Zigman, when inside and Wads in the buddy seat, keyed the ignition. He slammed the shifter down and floored the accelerator, squealing the cruiser away.

Zigman threw the car into a skid at the end of the driveway that took the car onto the state highway. He kept the accelerator on the floor, punching buttons that kicked on the siren and light bar. "Wads, get on the radio. Get us some help."

Wads snatched the microphone from its dash clip and pressed the transmit button. "Dispatch, Detective Zigman."

A woman's voice, a whiskey tenor, came back. "Go ahead, Zig."

"Zig's a bit busy. I'm his radioman, John Wads. We're pursuing a black Harley-Davidson."

"Wads, are you requesting help?"

"Got that right. We're westbound on State Seventy-three, ten miles east of Jimmytown. Get us a roadblock at the city limits."

"Can do. . . . All police cars, city and county, officer requests a roadblock on West Seventy-three at the city limits. Subject on a black Harley. Who's closest, respond?"

A siren came over the radio. "D'Haze, city patrolman, coming out of Wads's Kwik Trip. I can be there in a minute."

A second siren came over. "Deputy Montesinos, be there in three."

"Anyone behind Zig who can join the pursuit?"

A third voice joined the conversation. "Trooper Simon, just coming off the Interstate. I'm a couple miles back."

"You're number two, Trooper. . . . Wads, where are you now?"

Wads, one hand braced against the dash, brought his mic up. "About five out. Dammit, the biker's just cut off to the left. What road's there?"

"The map on my screen shows a one-lane gravel track going to Lake Kandiyah."

Zigman stomped down on the brakes. He slalomed through the turn-off and again stepped down on the gas, rocketing the cruiser across washboards and over potholes. "I've got the taillight. Oh, shit."

Wads looked up to see four headlights boring up the track.

Zigman threw the cruiser to the right, into the ditch and up the other side. He mowed down a forest of Sumac bushes as he held the cruiser parallel to the track. The opposing vehicle shot past, and Zigman wrenched the steering wheel to the left and brought the cruiser back up on the gravel. "You see the taillight?"

"No. Yes. Up ahead, going over a rise." Wads glanced across at the cruiser's speedometer. "Eighty? You out to kill us?"

"You'd be going faster."

"Because I'm a better driver, yeah."

The pulsing flash of the blue lights created unearthly shadows as the cruiser raced by scrub brush and pines that made a canyon of the gravel track, the siren wailing, nothing answering it, not even an echo.

Wads stared ahead. His eyes widened to saucer size. "Skunk!"

The cruiser thumped over a lone black and white animal meandering the road, crushing a cloud of stench from him.

Wads ran down his window. "My God, a direct hit."

Zigman hacked and wiped at his eye clouding up. "Is kinda bad."

"Kinda? You know how long it's gonna take to get this stink off me?"

Zigman refocused on the track. He careened down a dip and up the next rise, snuffling, scanning for the Harley's taillight. He caught it from the corner of his eye, the taillight retreating off to the left as his cruiser went airborne. To Wads, it seemed to be that he, Zigman, and the cruiser were suspended there between earth and the night sky for the longest time, until the cruiser splashed down in the shallows of a lake, slamming him and Zigman forward into the exploding airbags that slammed them back into the seat. They laid there, the air fizzing out of the bags.

Wads, when he recovered his voice, croaked out a "Zig, you all right?"

"Yeah, you?"

"Think so. I'm just laying here, you know, kinda trying to remember something."

"What?"

"Last winter, wasn't it, you put a car in the drink? Right, so this makes twice in less than a year. I'm wondering, Zig, are you goin' for a record?"

"Are you whining?"

"No, just thinking maybe next time I should drive."

"Can't. You're not a cop."

"I could be if you'd get the sheriff to hire me. . . . My shoes are getting wet, you know that? I can feel it."

"You are whining. Get out of my car!"

The radio crackled, followed by a series of clicks and "Dispatch to Zigman. Zig, you there?"

Zigman fumbled the microphone away from Wads and thumbed the transmit button. "Go ahead."

"You still in pursuit of the black motorcycle?"

"No."

"Got away?"

"You might say that. Whaddayah want?"

"Not a thing, but the deputies at the Deleatorre place, they want you back there. What's your location now?"

"The lake."

"Where about?"

"In it."

"Again?"

"You gonna get smart with me, too?"

Chapter 26

ZIGMAN MADE the turn into the Deleatorre driveway, a rear wheel of the mud-splattered cruiser thumping, as if the wheel were shaped like Humpty Dumpty. He drove on in silence, Wads in the buddy seat, his arms folded across his chest and he staring out the side window.

Zigman stopped under the portico.

A deputy, waiting by the front door, trotted out, only to back away. "What did you do to my cruiser?"

Zigman gave him the death stare.

"That stink. You hit a skunk?"

"Yes. I ran him down, deliberate. Homicide by motor vehicle. You wanted me back here?"

The deputy held out a gunmetal gray container the size of a cash box.

"So?"

"We found this in the search of the house. Deleatorre says it isn't his. We asked him if it was his wife's."

"And?"

"He said it might be. He doesn't have a key, and the box isn't on the search warrant."

Zigman turned to Wads.

"What, you're asking my opinion?"

Zigman waggled his trigger finger. "It looks to me like it could be a lock box for a gun. You agree?"

"So you are asking for my opinion."

"Yes."

"Zig, you've got a hand gun on the search warrant. I'd sure want to look inside." Wads held up a pocket-sized toolkit. "And I can pick the lock."

"You learn that in M.P. school?"

"No, from the Goldy Locks Locksmithing Home Study Course." Wads horsed himself out of the cruiser and into the night air.

Zigman greased his way out from behind the steering wheel. He motioned for the deputy to set the box on the hood of the cruiser. The deputy did and backpedaled away, upwind.

Wads leaned on the hood where he worked his picks into the lock. He twisted them in opposite directions, then twisted them a second time, and the lock, with a modest pop, gave up its security. Wads lifted the cover back, and Zigman shot a light in from his cellphone.

Wads raked his fingers back through his hair. "Bad news. No gun."

"Ah, but look at that fistful of papers. They're in plain sight, wouldn't you say? I can read those."

Wads took a black book from the box. "How about this?"

"What is it?"

"Got a lock on it, so I'd bet an Andrew Jackson it's either a diary or a journal."

"Whoa, a lock? Its contents are secured. They're not in plain sight."

"Which means you can't read what's in the book. But I can." Wads set to work with a single pick, snapping the lock open with a quick twist.

While he paged into the book, concluding it had to be a journal because none of the entries began with a 'Dear diary' salutation, Zigman sorted through the loose papers. He bumped Wads's elbow. "I've got a seventy-, seventy-one-year-old letter here from an Oldriska Moravek Doskocil. This has got to be the Oldriska Moravek who took Carrie Nation's hatchet to old Charlie's speakeasy back in the 'Thirties."

"Likely," Wads said without looking from his own reading.

"Doskocil? I'm thinking she and Deleatorre must be related. I'm beginning to get a picture here. And, oh, look at this." Zigman put his light on a center paragraph. "She says here Gilcrest raped her and murdered her sister, one Ivona Moravek. Says it was revenge for what they did to his place. The skull—female—we found in the cave, could that be Ivona?"

Zigman pulled a newspaper clipping up next. "Ah, an obit for the Doskocil woman dated February Sixteen, Two thousand. And jackpot. It lists her descendants, living and dead. Want to guess who's at the end of the list?"

Wads glanced up from the journal. "Anna Doskocil?"

"Give that man a gold star."

"Zig, I've got confirmation." Wads held the book over for Zigman to see, but jerked it back when he realized that would violate the search warrant. "Apparently, Anna as a little girl and Oldriska, her great grandma, were good buddies in the old woman's last years. On this page, Anna says she promised to be her great grandmother's avenging angel."

Zigman put the papers he had been reading back in the box. That done, he flicked up a finger. "So here's what we've got. One, Gilcrest rapes Oldriska and kills Ivona, both young women apparently temperance fanatics."

He flicked up a second finger. "Two, the rape produces a child. The letter says a son who, by the obit, is Anna Doskocil's grandfather."

He flicked up a third finger. "Three, the old woman wants her great granddaughter to take revenge for what happened to her."

Wads flipped forward in the journal a handful of pages. "Let's get up here to this year. Ah-ha, here's a note of interest."

Zigman waved his pinky. "Something for my fourth finger?"

"You're gonna like this. Anna writes here, 'June Eighteen, the Jamestown Herald today carried a story about a skull being found in a cave on the Gilcrest/Chrisco farm. Could that be my Great Aunt Ivona? If it is and I think it must be, I must avenge her death. I promised Great Grandma.'"

Chapter 27

WADS AND ZIGMAN strolled into the cave and back to the speakeasy where Chrisco sat at a table, working on a laptop. Beyond, a man in coveralls ran a buffer over the dance floor while others swept up debris left by the grand opening night's guests.

Wads and Zigman pulled up chairs and sat down. Chrisco peered over the screen at them, graying circles beneath his eyes. "All right, which one of you is wearing the bad cologne?"

Zigman pointed at Wads, and Wads at Zigman.

"Eau de Mephitis," Wads said.

Chrisco, puzzled, scratched at his sideburn.

"Mephitis," Wads repeated, "Pepe Le Pew, striped kitty cat. Zig hit one last night. He scrubbed himself with Lava soap to get it off, and I soaked in tomato juice."

"You may want to try again."

"Thanks."

Chrisco gave the eye to Zigman. "So did you catch her?"

He shook his head.

Wads came forward in his chair. "We've got an idea we want to lay on you."

Chrisco leaned to the side, the side of his face on his open hand, his elbow on the table. "Why am I not going to like this."

"Because you could get killed."

"That is something I would not like."

"Look, Count, she got away. She's in the wind. She knows she can come after you again."

"I liked the girl, Wads. That's why I hired her. Why doesn't she like me?"

"Because she's a temperance nut, plus you're operating where Gilcrest murdered her great aunt."

"What's this about a great aunt?"

"The skull we found in your cave back in the spring, Anna's great aunt. And Zig came on a letter in Anna's lock box confirming that Gilcrest killed the woman."

"My God."

"You're in the line of fire, my friend, and Zig and I want to control that line." Wads sucked in a breath. When the airline pilot-slash-saloon owner held his silence, listening, Wads thumbed to Zigman.

Zigman folded his hands together. "Chrisco, we want you to have a second grand opening."

Chrisco rotated his hand in a keep-going gesture.

"We want you to have a masked ball, everyone to come in costume."

"Hmm, now this gets my interest. Could be a helluva promotion scheme here."

"Yes, and Anna Deleatorri's going to see it as a perfect opportunity to get in here, kill you, and get away. She'll come."

"If she does, how're you going to keep her from killing me?"

Wads patted the tabletop. "Easy, my friend. We'll have a photo station that everyone has to pass through. We'll tell people as they arrive at the station that you're having pictures taken of everyone to post on Facebook, Twitter, and Instagram, you know, pictures with their masks on and pictures with their masks off. If Anna comes and takes her mask off, Zig will grab her."

"And if she refuses to take her mask off?"

"Now wouldn't that be suspicious? Zig will grab her anyway."

Chapter 28

WADS AND LARSON, Wads dressed as The Old Actor from "The Fantasticks," complete with frizzled white hair, and Larson as a short-skirted Little Red Riding Hood, leaned together with Zigman, he in the get-up of Fagan from "Oliver," the three off to the side of the photo station.

Zigman pulled out a pocket watch and considered the time. "Nobody's come through for a while. I'd say everybody who's coming is here, wouldn't you?"

Wads checked his own watch. "And no Anna-the-shooter."

On stage, Jack Farina's Big Band hit the drum riff for The Beach Boys' "Wipe Out," emptying the tables as costumed guests swarmed onto the dance floor.

Wads pitched up his voice. "Looks like our plan was a dud."

Zigman cupped a hand behind his ear.

"I said it looks like our plan's a dud!"

Larson clasped Wads's hand. "Maybe not." She gave a toss of her head at a waiter with short black hair and a mustache, carrying a tray of hors d'oeuvres toward Zigman at the end of the bar. "Check out his butt."

Wads glanced that way. "What about it?"
"See how wide it is in relation to the shoulders?"
"Yeah?"
"It isn't a guy. It's a woman."
"With a mustache?"
"It's a fake. It's good, but it's a fake. Are you gonna stand here sucking your thumb?"

Wads and Zigman raised their eyebrows in unison and together moved out, hustling after the waiter. Wads saw her set the tray on the bar and in a fluid motion bring a pistol out from under her jacket. The waiter jammed the muzzle into Chrisco's chest. In an instant, he fell back and down.

Zigman whipped out his weapon, a Glock Nine, as he kicked into high gear. He raced toward Chrisco.

Wads, with his Beretta held high, charged after the shooter running toward the kitchen. He cut left and burst through a secondary door into the side cave. There he snapped on the floodlights.

The shooter slammed through the door beyond Wads, from the storeroom behind the kitchen. She ran on toward the far end where she stopped hard, jerking her head from side to side, panicked by a different arrangement of the rocks at the end of the cave and a sign hand-lettered in magic marker: NO EXIT. GO DIRECTLY TO JAIL. DO NOT PASS GO. DO NOT COLLECT $200.

She wheeled around.

Wads, crouched by the storeroom door, raised his gun. He aimed it at her. "Anna, nice disguise."

"Who's that?"

"John Wads, your old dance partner. Anna, this is where it ends. What do you want to do?"

"Get away from here."

"Not gonna happen."

"At least I killed that evil Chrisco, didn't I?"

"What's evil about him?"

"He pushed liquor on people. And he bought this place where my great aunt was murdered. He bought it. I had to avenge her death."

"Anna, he's not dead."

She squinted at Wads, he behind the hottest area of the lights. "I don't believe you."

"We put him in a flak jacket. Lay your gun down, and I'll take you out and you can see for yourself."

"No, I don't believe you." Deleatorre shifted a pace to the side, her weapon, a Sig Sauer, tight in both hands held out straight, targeted on Wads. She pursed her lips and brought her weapon up, turning the muzzle as she did back toward her face.

Startled, Wads squeezed off a shot.

Deleatorre crumpled, a red stain appearing on the leg of her tux trousers, spreading as she fell.

Wads sprang up and raced to her, kicked her gun away and knelt beside her. He shucked himself out of his vest and packed it around the wound. "Just be glad I'm not a cop. They're trained to shoot at your body mass, at your chest. You'd be dead, missy."

She gasped, shock going to pain. "I'd be off better dead."

"Don't think your husband would see it that way." He clamped Deleatorri's hand over the unglamourous bandage. "Hold this."

As she did, Wads ripped the sleeve from his costume's shirt. "Missy, I grew up on a farm. I'm a hunter, a crack shot. I hit what I aim for, and I aimed for your leg." He whipped the sleeve around the bandage, tied a knot and hauled down tight on it, Deleatorri's face twisting, tears coursing from the corners of her eyes.

"Can't you let me die?"

"You'll have to have a more serious wound than this."

"Then shoot me again, please."

"Sorry. Missy, your husband's a nice guy. He's got too much money, but he's a nice guy. It's time you thought about him, what he'd want if he were here, don'tcha think?"

Addendum

What follows are pertinent materials from the case file:

Letter from Oldriska Moravek, the original written in pencil on lined paper.
June 14, 1943
To my son, may you not read this before I am dead,
    I want you to know some things about me that have never been talked about, including who your real father is.
    When I was much younger, I led a group of temperance women from my church who attacked and destroyed much of the interior of an underground saloon on the Charles Gilcrest farm. We were protesting the liquor it served and the harm it was doing to the men of our families who patronized the saloon.
    None of us attempted to hide our identities. As a consequence, Mister Gilcrest filed a complaint against us. When we made it clear we looked forward to facing him in court, he swore revenge. Two nights later, he kidnapped me and your aunt who you've never met, my sister, Ivona. He beat me terribly, had his way with me and left me for dead in a room in his

house, though I was conscious, barely. He then beat Ivona. When she fought back, he shot her. After he carried her body from the room to where I do not know, I dragged myself out of there and into the woods where I hid.

Sometime later, after I had enough strength, I limped away. I knew I could not go home for Mister Gilcrest might find me there, so I walked to Tesda, to the home of my cousin Magda Chlebek. She and her husband, Hieronym, agreed to hide me. I stayed with them until I read the newspaper story that Mister Gilcrest had disappeared. Only then did I go home, and I had you in my belly.

You were born without a father. To the priest, that was a sin that could not be forgiven. When he told my father and my mother that I must leave the church, my father told him that was casting a stone in judgement, that God could not forgive that, that it was a far greater sin. The priest became angry and told us we must all leave, and we did, and our friends with us, almost half the congregation.

The next year I met a very fine man, a temperance man, Anton Doskocil. He married me in a Methodist Church and adopted you. This is the man you knew as your father. Before the war came, he joined the Army National Guards, the 192nd Tank Battalion. His unit was called up, and he died on Bataan in the Philippine Islands. You were eight years old.

Your father.

But your real father was Charles Gilcrest. I know so little about him and want to know no more.

Your loving mother,
Oldriska Moravek Doskocil

Oldriska Moravek Doskocil's obituary
Jamestown Herald
February 16, 2000

Bratz — Oldriska Moravek Doskocil, age 98, died at the Bratz Convalescent Home on February 12 of natural causes.

She was predeceased by her husband of seven years, Anton Doskocil, a member of the Army National Guards' 192nd Tank Battalion, who was killed in 1942 at the Battle of Bataan.

She was also predeceased by her only son, Frantisek "Frank" Doskocil, who was killed July 24, 1962, in a skirmish with the Viet Cong near Darlac, South Vietnam. Doskocil, a member of the U.S. Army Special Forces, was age 33 at the time of his death.

Mrs. Doskocil is survived by one grandson, Edvard "Eddie" Doskocil, 34, of rural Jamestown, and one great granddaughter, Anna Doskocil, 11, also of rural Jamestown.

The funeral is set for today (February 16) at 2 p.m. at the Saint Procopius Catholic Church of Bratz with interment to follow in the Saint Procopius Cemetery.

Excerpts from Anna Doskocil's journal
July 26, 1997

Today was my great grandmother's birthday. She is 92. I cannot imagine how old that must be. My father and I took her a small cake. No one else ever visits her. Other relatives say she's crazy, even my mother, but I think she's nice. We tell each other such great stories, but only when my father is not in the room, and that's often because he has a friend of his father's in the nursing home that he also likes to visit. Great Grandma calls me her angel.

Today she asked me if I had ever read the letter she had wrote to her son, who would be my grandfather. It was all about the terrible things that happened to her when she was a young woman and a leader of our church's temperance society. She had to explain what temperance was to me, and made me promise to never drink wine or beer or anything else like that, that those things are evil.

I said I had not seen the letter, and she said I should find it, that it must be in the box she had given to her son and that it must have come to my father when his mother, my grandmother, died. It could be in the attic. I promised to look for it.

July 28, 1997

I found Great Grandma Oldriska's letter today. It was horrible, about the things a Mr. Gilcrest did to her and how he killed Great Grandma's sister.

August 2, 1997

I showed Great Grandma the letter today when my father was not in the room. She told me that I should keep it forever, that I should hide it with my journal and that one day I should be her avenging angel, that she would tell me what I should do.

June 18, 2014

The Jamestown Herald today carried a story about a skull being found in a cave on the Gilcrest/Chrisco farm. Could that be my Great Aunt Ivona? If it is, and I believe it is, I must avenge her death. I promised Great Grandma.

ABOUT THE AUTHOR

Jerry Peterson writes crime novels set in Kansas, Tennessee, and now with *Iced* and *Rubbed Out*, in Wisconsin.

Before becoming a writer, Peterson taught speech, English and theater in Wisconsin high schools, then worked in communications for farm organizations for a decade in Wisconsin, Michigan, Kansas and Colorado.

He followed that with a decade as a reporter, photographer, and editor for newspapers in Colorado, West Virginia, Virginia, and Tennessee.

Today, he lives and writes in his home state of Wisconsin, the land of brats, beer, and good books.

UPCOMING TITLES

Coming next year, *Rooster's Story*, the third book in my series of Wings Over the Mountains novels. Rooster Wilhite, a pursuit pilot in The Great War, loses an arm in an accident years after the war. After a difficult recuperation, he discovers he can still fly airplanes, so signs on to fly the airmail in the early and dangerous days of night flight.

Made in the USA
Charleston, SC
09 November 2014